THE UTAH KID

THE UTAH KID

ROE RICHMOND

CUTTING EDGE

Previously published as *The Conestoga Cowboy*.

ISBN-13: 978-1-954840-16-4

Published by
Cutting Edge Books
PO Box 8212
Calabasas, CA 91372
www.cuttingedgebooks.com

CHAPTER ONE

In the River Belle saloon and gambling house they were talking about Sherrill. For several weeks the name of this young man had figured prominently in the conversations of Bedloe Landing. Today they could talk freely because Jay Lavery, owner of the establishment, was keeping his bruised face out of sight, and his three chief gunmen, Mitchum, Holway and Dakin, had withdrawn to a far corner table.

"Sherry shoulda killed Lavery last night," was one opinion. "Beatin' his head half off ain't goin' to get Sherry anythin' but grief. Lavery's sure to get him now. He'll have the boys out after him before sundown. They been strainin' at the leash for some spell."

"They better be sharp when they go for Sherry," said another. "I never saw nothin' like Sherry that night he took them two gamblers in the Royal. Hinsman an' Dobbs was slick, too. Sherry took 'em like a short drink."

"That was sure enough somethin'," agreed a third. "Seems like comin' up-river on the Mississippi Maid, Sherry cleaned them two. When they put in to the Landin', this Hinsman an' Dobbs hung around till they figgered Sherry was drunk in the Royal. He's at the bar, an' they come in an' brace him one on each side. I'm tellin' you lightnin' never struck no faster. Sherry shot 'em both dead, one slug from each gun. Hinsman was still reachin', an' Dobbs had his iron half out. They couldn't believe it, even with the lead in 'em. I wouldn'ta believed it if I hadn't been

1

there. Harry Connover's seen 'em all. He claims he never saw a better man than Sherry with the Colts."

"Don't forget these boys of Lavery's are good, too," interposed the first speaker. " 'Specially Holway an' the Preacher. An' they'll be about six to one, if Lavery sends 'em all."

"He better send 'em all if he wants any back alive!"

"Funny, that Sherrill ain't much to look at. Never take him for a killer. Just a kid, a kinda pretty boy with bright hair an' a grin you can't help likin'. But he don't give a hoot in Hades for nothin'."

"He's got a name down the river. I heard about him in Natchez an' Memphis, him an' another young heller called Patch. Hellfire behind that easy smile, an' women crazy for him all the way down to New Orleans."

"A woman is all that keeps him alive here. Wasn't for Lilli Lavery, he woulda been buried weeks back. Dunno why, but Jay won't let nobody take Sherrill long as he stands in with Lil. Danged funny way for a man to be with his wife, but that's how it is."

"Sherry ain't goin' to rate so high with Lilli neither. Not when she hears about him walkin' outa here last night with Nina Montez, after losin' all his money an' knocking the stuffin' outa Jay."

"If Lil turns on him Sherry better breeze outa Bedloe. When that comes Jay'll turn loose Mitchum, Holway, Dakin, the whole pack. Sherry ain't that good he can take 'em all."

The group glanced covertly at the corner table where the gunmen sulked. The boys weren't happy about having their boss beaten up in his own place. Mitchum, dressed entirely in black, had the gaunt, hollow-cheeked face and brooding, sorrowful, half mad eyes of a mountain preacher. Holway was big and brawny but easy-moving, his scarred face hard, insolent and tough, a chew of tobacco bulging one jaw. Dakin was thin and wiry with the sneering face of a shark. They were all ruthless killers, a notorious and terrible trio. And for a long time they had been waiting to get at Sherrill.

"No," said the last speaker thoughtfully. "Sherry ain't that good."

At approximately the same time, Sherrill emerged from the back door of an adobe-block house near the outskirts of town, a structure somewhat larger and more pretentious than its neighbors. Laughing, he crossed the narrow porch, swung over the rail and dropped lightly to the ground. As he ducked down the alley a small-calibered pistol cracked spitefully from the doorway, and splinters stung his cheek as the bullet screamed off the wall.

Sherrill jogged out of the alleyway to the next street, smiling and shaking his head. He was long and lean and limber, his hair and eyes the color of whiskey, his face boyish and clear, almost delicate. That had been rather close, closer no doubt than Lilli intended, although she was raging. "Hell hath no fury," he murmured, pausing at the corner to roll and light a cigarette.

Lilli Lavery had finally learned of his occasional meetings with Nina Montez, long her rival in the night life of the river port, and the repercussions were apt to be anything but laughable.

It was time, Sherrill realized, that he get away from Bedloe Landing. His money was gone, his luck had changed, and he knew from experience that he was in for a bad run now. With him it was either way up or way down; never halfway, moderate, normal, never any happy medium. Either he couldn't lose or it was impossible to win. He had hit the heights in this town, and now he was on the way down. The time had come to move. The question was where and how.

Sherrill sauntered along the rutted street with dust rising from the traffic of horsemen, wagons and buckboards, past rude houses of sod, plank and brick toward the central plaza and the river. Flat-crowned hat tilted rakishly, he was slim and elegant in scarlet satin shirt, gray scarf, gray trousers, expensive Star boots, the gun belt with its two sheathed Colts binding his flat hips.

Here and there people greeted him and turned to look after him. There were offers of rides in a variety of creaking, rumbling vehicles which he declined politely. Sherrill had been in Bedloe only a month and he was already a legend. His second night in town he had broken the bank in both Harry Connover's Royal and Jay Lavery's River Belle, and the famous beauty Lilli had selected him as her own. Today his pockets were empty, and Lilli had just tried to shoot him. Things had indeed come to a pretty pass.

Now Sherrill craved a drink but lacked the price. He had expected to retrieve some of last night's losses from Lil, but she had preferred to pay him off in lead this afternoon. Women were funny all right. He started singing in a low, clear voice:

> *"You may talk of Sue and Molly,*
> *But I've one that's got 'em beat,*
> *She's my little hot tamale,*
> *Just as hot as she is sweet."*

At the head of the square, Sherrill halted indecisively and shaped another cigarette, his amber eyes roving over the milling and motley throngs. There were farmers and homesteaders in homespun, cowboys in plain or colorful range garb, lumberjacks with calked boots and plaid shirts, frontiersmen in buckskin, gamblers in black-and-white broadcloth, and drifters wearing anything from Eastern store clothes to back-woods rags.

On the left was the River Belle, and Sherrill contemplated entering in search of Nina Montez and a few dollars, but decided against it. Jay Lavery may have given his gunhands the word already. Holway's trigger finger itched every time he saw Sherrill anyway, while Dakin looked more than ever like a hungry shark, and Mitchum's cadaverous countenance assumed an expression of mournful piety that foretold killing. They'd get to Sherrill quickly enough without his walking in and asking for it. He wasn't in a fighting mood or ready for the showdown.

On his right was the Royal, and Harry Connover, the proprietor, would be glad to lend him money, although Harry was certain to gibe him about losing to Lavery. But Sherrill had always found it easier to accept money from women than from men. Wondering idly why this was so, he concluded that he must be without moral fiber and character. It did not bother him much to assay his shortcomings. Nothing mattered a great deal since his family had been wiped out, his father and elder brother dying with Stuart before Spottsylvania, his mother and sister murdered by marauding guerrillas.

Across the way stood the Queen's Hotel in which Sherrill had a seldom used room. The hotel, with the River Belle and the Royal, dominated the plaza. Lesser structures of adobe, brick and plank housed other saloons, stores and markets, harness shops and livery stables, a bank, dance hall, blacksmith's forge, feed and grain mill, barber shop, all mushroomed together in heterogeneous confusion, all more or less busy.

Briefly Sherrill wondered what it would be like to work for a living. In moments of depression he sometimes envied men with steady jobs, until comprehension of the dullness and monotony of routine labor appalled his senses. No, that was not for him.... What was it Patchin used to say? "Only fools and horses work, and horses back up to it." Patchin, with those twinkling blue eyes and that broad homely grin, had been a good partner until he had married that girl in Memphis. Poor Patch, he must be working now.... At any rate, he had got a fine girl in Veronica. Even so, Sherry thought of him almost as if he were dead.

He crossed the square and strolled on down Front Street toward the river. He could sign on one of the side-wheelers as a house gambler, he supposed, but he didn't like the idea of sharing his profits. And with his luck on the downgrade, there probably wouldn't be any profits to share, and the captain would bounce him off at the first stop. Sherrill smiled whimsically. Even that would get him out of Bedloe Landing, away from Lilli and Nina, away from Jay Lavery and his hired guns.

At the rim of the bluff Sherrill made another smoke and stood staring out over the docks and the broad sweep of the Mississippi River. Traffic had been heavy of late and the Landing a boom town. On the flats were the wagons and tents of the emigrants preparing to start their long trek westward. He had met a few of them—the Romneys and fat jovial Ed Deal were the ones he remembered—and Sherrill felt sorry for them. Men burdened down with whole families pushing out to make homes in the wilderness.

They had a tremendous battle against overwhelming odds on their hands, complicated by the presence of so many women and children. There was heat and thirst and hunger to face, as well as the hostile Indians. There were endless plains, deserts and the Rocky Mountains to be crossed. Death stalked close to every wagon train west.... Sherrill marveled at the courage, or foolhardiness, of men who led their wives and children into such a venture. It was hard enough for a man alone to stand up and fight this raw, primitive Western world.

A man by himself could endure a lot before breaking, but when he was forced to watch his womenfolk and kids suffer and die, disintegration, despair and madness were apt to set in. Sherrill shook his head and tried to dismiss the matter. It was their problem, not his; he had troubles of his own. Let them go out and die in the desert if they chose. He felt sorry for the women and children, but they were none of his business.... Since Spottsylvania and the pillaging of a certain Southern manor, human life had diminished in value, so far as Sherrill was concerned.

CHAPTER TWO

Walking back toward town, Sherrill met the Romney brothers, Whitmore and Judson. "Well, boys," he said, smiling in response to their eager, "Hello, Sherry!" Sherrill had felt a strong instinctive liking for them from the first, and it was mutual. They were nearly as tall as his six feet one, stalwart and keen and supple, a fine looking pair. Whit, blond and gray-eyed, with a quick boyish smile that dimpled one brown cheek, was built on slender, graceful lines. Jud, somewhat stockier and graver, had black hair and brown eyes. But their smiles were identical, their pleasant bronzed features similar, and they might have been twins with contrasting coloring.

"When are you pulling out?" inquired Sherrill.

"In the morning," answered Whit Romney. "Why don't you come along with us, Sherry? We might need you to fight off the Apaches."

Sherrill grinned. "I've got nothing against the Indians."

"You would have," Judson said grimly, "if you'd seen what they do to some wagon trains!"

"I know, Jud," said Sherrill gently. "But I'm no pioneer. Maybe I'm too fond of comfort."

Whitmore laughed. "From what we hear, you won't be getting much comfort in Bedloe, Sherry!"

"Is the news out already? I'll have to seek the protection of Sheriff Slocumb."

Even the sober Jud laughed aloud, the law being what it was in Bedloe Landing. Whit said: "Sherry, you better come down and say goodbye to Mother and Dad. They haven't forgotten how you took care of them that time in the hotel."

"That was nothing," Sherrill protested. "Your dad could have handled those drunks all right. I just didn't want to see your mother embarrassed."

"Besides, Sis is dying to meet you," grinned Whit.

"Too bad to disillusion a young girl," Sherrill drawled. "Would you boys buy me a drink first? I had a bad run last night."

"It'll be an honor," Jud assured him gravely, and they headed at once into the smoke-hazed din of the nearby Waterfront Saloon. Midway through their second round, they were joined by Ed Deal, a massive man with a laughing red face, powerful in spite of the fat he carried.

"You decided to come along and see the great West, Sherry?" he boomed. "We can use a lad like you out there."

"Afraid not, Ed. I don't think Lavery'd like it if I left town. Which trail you taking?"

"Salt Lake, and it ain't bad at all. Independence, Kearney, Fort Laramie, and over the hump to Bridger."

"Who's scouting for you?"

"Fiddle Filchock." Deal saw Sherry's look and asked: "Is that bad?"

"No, the Fiddler'll be all right when he sobers up."

Ed Deal grunted. "He better had. Macklin'll flog the liquor outa him with that whip o' his."

"Trail boss?"

"Yeah." Deal peered around rather furtively. "Don't like the man much myself. But he's got guts, he's a driver, and that's what you need. Macklin's got a coupla tough boys to help him, too: Koogle and Spicer."

Whit Romney grimaced. "Too tough—they think."

"Well, it's a rough business," Ed Deal said.

After several rounds they left Ed at the bar and went out to descend the slope toward the encampment on the river flats.

Sherrill was feeling better as they passed through long lines of wagons: sway-backed Conestogas, high old chuckwagons, sturdy Pittsburghs, and huge Murphys. Children were playing among the tents and wagons, shooting Indians, adding their shrill cries to the bawling of cattle. Everyone semed to know and like the Romney brothers, hailing them from all sides. There was such a festive air about the camp that Sherrill wondered if these people had any conception of what lay ahead of them. Perhaps it was fully as well if they did not.

The brothers, in the way of boys, were a trifle impatient here while Sherrill chatted with their mother and father. Mrs. Romney was tall for a woman, with a proud head of graying hair, deep faded gray eyes, fine features, and a gracious manner. Mr. Romney, a bit shorter than his six-foot sons, was built broad, compact and solid. A grave, quiet, pipe-smoking man, with thinning fair hair, mild brown eyes, and a strong-boned face that was distinctive. They were soft-spoken, friendly and gentle, but there was courage and will underneath. Sherrill was surprised to learn that they came from Vermont. He had never suspected there were people of such quality among the Yankees.

Whit finally grabbed Sherrill's arm. "Come and see the wagon, Sherry. It's a beauty."

It was shining clean and bright, a Conestoga, red-wheeled and blue-bodied, with a yellow hood. Sherrill expressed proper appreciation but his eyes were more for the horses. There were six for the wagon and five saddle horses, all prime sleek specimens, and Sherrill contemplated what an investment this outfit must constitute. The Romneys certainly were well equipped for the journey, far better than most of their companions, many of whom had oxen and mules.

Everything the family possessed was thrown into this cross-continental quest, a much greater gamble than any Sherrill had ever undertaken.... They were looking at the horses when the girl came up. Whit introduced her, and Sherrill suffered a shock that tingled through his entire being, caught at his throat and took his breath away, leaving him dazed, shaken and lightheaded.

Molly Romney had rich burnished dark hair and wide gray eyes in a tanned face so pure and flawless it struck through him like a steel blade. She was slim, straight and lissome, but full-breasted and superbly curved in the simple dress she was wearing because it would be so long a time before she could dress like a woman again. There was a clean freshness about her that made blonde Lilli Lavery and dark Nina Montez look like what they undoubtedly were: a pair of painted trollops. Molly's glance was frank and straight, she had the warm, bright Romney smile, and her voice was soft flowing music.

"So you're Sherry. I'm glad to meet you at last."

For once in his life Sherrill was tongue-tied, feeling absurdly young and raw and awkward, painfully conscious of his scarlet shirt and the heavy guns dragging at his thighs. Somehow he felt unworthy and ashamed. There was a humility in him that he had not known since standing before his mother in boyhood. He swallowed hard but could not speak. With one accord they turned and moved a little way toward the river.

"I'm glad you came," Molly said. "I was afraid I wouldn't see you at all."

At last words came, but with difficulty. "The pleasure is mine. I think a lot of your brothers. Your folks are fine, too."

Molly Romney laughed lightly. "The boys worship you, Sherry. Dad and Mother were quite impressed, too. They've all been hoping you'd join the train." When Sherrill shook his head slowly she went on: "Is there anything in Bedloe Landing worth staying and perhaps dying for?"

"No, but it's my kind of life."

"Don't you get tired of it? I've seen those places and those people...."

"Sure. But I'd get more tired of crawling across the plains."

"You like excitement, don't you?" She studied him closely.

Sherrill nodded. "That's about all there is for me, I guess."

"If you have to use those guns," Molly Romney murmured, "I should think you'd want to do some good with them."

"That can be done right here at the Landing," Sherrill smiled.

"It could be done a lot better by protecting the lives of women and children."

"That's right," agreed Sherrill. "But I'm no Indian fighter."

Molly sighed. "All right, Sherry, I'm sorry." She turned back toward where her brothers were waiting impatiently. Dark Judson was scowling and kicking the turf, while blond Whitmore concentrated on forming a cigarette.

"I'm the one to be sorry," Sherrill said, pacing beside her. "I'd like to go, but I don't belong here. Not with people like you and your family … I didn't know there were families like this in wagon trains."

"Why, yes, Sherry." She smiled up at him. "We're the backbone of the country. Didn't you know?"

Sherrill bowed his red-gold head. "The country's all right then. The country will live."

"You could help it. You *could* belong if you wanted to."

"Not any more. It's too late, Miss Romney."

"Hey, Sherry!" Jud called gruffly, almost sullenly. "I need another drink before supper."

"You're talked me into it, Judson," said Sherrill. "Let's go."

Molly said: "You're easily talked into some things, I see."

"Any of the vices," Sherrill said soberly. "Miss Romney, I can't quite say …" He held out his hand, and the girl took it.

"You don't have to," Molly said gently. "I know."

They stood there until the brothers called again, and Sherry turned after them with a mixture of relief and regret, troubled by the surge of emotion the girl had aroused in him. He had known many women, but not one had ever made him feel this way. He was startled and upset, stunned and incredulous. *Molly*

Romney.... And she was leaving in the morning. He would never see her again.

As they neared the edge of camp a man crossed to intercept them with an air of swaggering authority. A big man, no taller than Sherrill, but much broader and heavier, with tremendous shoulders and arms. There was arrogance in his stride and contempt in his dark, hard-set hawk-face. Sherry bristled with instinctive dislike even before the man spoke.

"Howdy, boys. Who's your friend here?"

There never could be anything humble about the Romneys, but there was some slight deference in their manner as they presented Sherry to Cord Macklin. The big man carried a thick, heavy quirt in his right hand, flicking it now and then with a powerful practiced wrist. His strangely glittering black eyes were insolent as they swept Sherrill from hat to boots, lingering on the satin shirt and the gun belt.

"Yeah, I've heard of him," Cord Macklin said. "What's he doin' here?"

Whit Romney's fair face colored. "Wait a minute, Cord!"

"No offense, Whit," said Cord Macklin. "I understand a new outfit's joinin' up with us, and I'm checkin' on 'em. Thought maybe your friend was with 'em, see?"

Sherrill had had enough of this. "Well, I'm not," he said. "And if I were, what would it be to you?"

Cord Macklin laughed unpleasantly and cracked the whip like a shot. "I'm bossin' this wagon train, that's all. I'm kinda particular who rides with it. Any objections, mister?"

"I'm not interested," said Sherrill, anger stirring and rising hotly in him. "Neither in you nor your wagon train. Come on, boys."

Macklin moved enough to bar his path. "Only in the Romneys, huh?" The sarcasm was heavy.

"That's right," Sherrill said, stepping toward him. "Out of the way now. I don't usually take this much from any man."

Cord Macklin stood his ground, swinging his quirt and eyeing Sherry's guns. "I know you're a gun-fighter. I wonder if you're any good without them guns?"

"You can find out," Sherrill told him. "Drop that quirt and I'll drop my gun belt."

Cord Macklin laughed and made the quirt sing. "This little whip has come close to cuttin' gun-hands off at the wrist."

Sherrill smiled. "I use either hand."

"In that case I'd work on your neck—or eyes." Macklin stood solid and sure, measuring his man.

"Try it," invited Sherrill, lounging loose and easy, slender and boyish before that rugged bulk.

There was hatred between them, springing instantaneously from unknown depths, burning with an intensity that would last as long as they lived. For a tense moment they stood face to face, watchful and, waiting, poised to strike. Then it was broken by the jarring mockery of Macklin's laughter and the cold rasp of his voice:

"If I see you around here again I will!" He strode back toward the wagons, cutting the air with hissing strokes of the lash. Sherrill's amber eyes followed him intently.

"Come on, Sherry," said Jud Romney. "I'm dryer'n ever."

"Nice sociable fellow," commented Sherrill as they went on toward the bluff.

Whit laughed uneasily. "Cord isn't generally that bad. He saw you talking to Molly and it made him sore."

"Oh." Sherry tried to make it casual. "He got a claim there?"

"Not exactly," grinned Whit. "But he'd sure like to have."

"Well, you can't blame him for that," Sherrill drawled. "Your sister is a pretty sweet girl."

"Sure, she's all right," Whit said without enthusiasm.

"That quirt is a new one on me," admitted Sherrill.

"Cord's really dynamite with that whip," Jud said. "He blinded a gunman in Natchez, and crippled another one's gun-wrist on the boat."

"That poor guy in Natchez," Whit said. "He came at Macklin over some woman trouble. Cord caught him square across the eyes. Cord's awful fast with that blasted thing."

"Nice fellow," smiled Sherrill, patting the gun-handles on his thighs. "But I'll string along with these."

CHAPTER THREE

An hour and a number of drinks later Sherrill parted with the Romney brothers outside the Waterfront, declining their invitation to supper on the grounds that he did not care for whipping with his meals. They offered to stay uptown with him, but he wouldn't listen to it. The boys finally said they might get away and look him up later that night, and Sherry told them he hoped they would.

Walking toward the center of town with no definite objective in mind, Sherrill kept an eye out for Lavery's gun-sharps. If Lilli had given the thumbs-down sign, they would be gunning for him, and the top three, Mitchum, Holway and Dakin, were not to be underestimated. Sherrill's reason for not accepting the Romney invitation to supper was a reluctance to place himself once more under the compelling spell of Molly's charm. If he had lived a decent kind of life he might have gone on to court and marry Molly Romney. As it was, he had to let her go without a word.... Sherrill tried to shrug it off. Too late now to change, too late to be sorry. But the sense of loss and emptiness and futility persisted. With his luck running downhill, he was always inclined to be morbid.

Four different men along Front Street informed Sherrill that Harry Connover wanted to see him in the Royal. A feeling of foreboding grew in him as he neared the square, where oil lamps were beginning to glimmer in the early dusk. Knowing he should eat something, although he had no appetite, he stopped in a little restaurant for a sandwich and coffee, sitting back against the wall so he could watch the entrance. Afterward he fashioned a cigarette and sat for a space smoking thoughtfully, troubled by a loneliness that he was unused to and that he did not like. Meeting Molly Romney had made him dissatisfied with everything, particularly himself.

Sherrill was striding along the slat sidewalk with alert eyes probing the shadows when a woman's voice reached him through the crowd: "Sherry!" Hungry-eyed men watched narrowly as Nina Montez ran up and clung to Sherrill's arm, her dark eyes lifted anxiously to his clear face.

"They are after you, Sherry," she said with the precise curious accent that once had delighted him. "All of them. Lavery has set them loose. That jealous wife of his, of course. Sherry, you must take care!"

"I always do," he said shortly, looking at her rouge and earrings with faint distaste, attempting to free his arm without offending her. After seeing Molly Romney, he had no desire to be with Nina or Lilli Lavery or any of their sort. But Nina retained her grip firmly.

"You come with me now, Sherry."

"I can't go with you. I've got to see Harry."

Nina shook his arm with impatience. "First you come with me. Harry knows of it; he sent me to find you. Come, Sherry."

"What's it all about?"

"A friend of yours wants you. A friend who is hurt."

"Who is it, Nina? Don't be so mysterious," Sherrill said.

"I don't know. I only know he is hurt and asking for you, Sherry. He came today on the boat. I have been taking care of him. Sometimes he sounds a little crazy in the head."

"All right, where is he?" Sherrill finally disengaged his arm and tried his guns in their holsters. Anything could be a trap now.

Nina Montez slanted a dark, scornful glance at him. "You don't trust me? You think I am another Lilli? Come, foolish boy."

Guffaws of bawdy laughter followed them as Nina led him toward the plaza and turned down a darkening alley. They came out behind a harness shop near the Royal. The main floor was dark, but light showed vaguely in the basement storeroom. Nina went down wooden steps and quietly opened the door to an odor of oiled leather. Sherrill drew his right-hand gun and trailed her into the dim room hung with harnesses and saddles. Nina closed the door and stood by it, pointing to an improvised bunk in the far corner.

"Let me take that gun, Sherry," she said. "I'll wait here."

Sherrill handed her the big .44 and brushed through a thin screen of leather straps. Lamplight from a single wall bracket flicked over the figure of a man stretched on his back, arms at sides, a bandage over his eyes, his body motionless. Sherrill advanced wonderingly, thinking the man was dead until he saw the dry lips move. The bandage covered the upper face completely, but Sherrill recognized something familiar in that stubborn cleft chin and wide mouth, the broken nose that had been broken again, by the look of it.

"Patch!" he said. "Patch boy, is it you?"

The broad mouth curved into that remembered homely grin. "It's me, Sherry. What's left of me." He held up both hands, and Sherrill gripped them hard.

"What they been doing to you, Patch?" Still holding Patchin's hands, Sherrill sat down on a crate beside the rude pallet.

"I'm all right, Sherry—except my eyes. I'm sure glad you're here, kid. I had to find you."

"What happened anyway, Patch?"

"Quite a story. Make me a cigarette and I'll tell you."

Sherrill rolled two cigarettes, lit them, and placed one between Patchin's lips. Patch inhaled with deep satisfaction. "It's a lie you can't taste tobacco smoke without seeing it."

Inside, Sherrill was boiling like a cauldron as a horrible suspicion took root and formed in his brain. Patchin's eyes had been the most remarkable thing about him, bright blue and brimming with gaiety and laughter in the old days. "There's a devil in your eyes, Patch," Veronica used to say. "A man with eyes like that is not to be trusted." But she could trust Patchin all right. He had forsaken all the old reckless, riotous, hell-to-breakfast ways and settled right down after marrying her.

"First, I lost Veronica," Patch said evenly through his teeth. Sherrill's own teeth were on edge and sweat started in his palms and armpits as he watched his shadow waver grotesquely on the wall. "I was away hauling freight for McClintock and Durfee," Patch went on. "These men musta seen Veronica on the street and followed her home. Our house was out a ways, no very near neighbors. I used to worry some, but Veronica always said she could take care of herself, and you remember how we taught her to handle a gun and shoot.

"I don't know how it happened, of course. I found out after there were three men, but one in particular.... They musta caught her by surprise, before she could get hold of a gun. When I got home she was gone and I found this note. She didn't want to live after that. Said she couldn't go on living.... About a week later they pulled her out of the river, ten miles downstream.

"I got a line on the men and lit out after them. The big one was the one I wanted most. Caught up with 'em in Natchez. Called the big one, had him under my gun, cold. But I wanted him to know what he was dying for, so I did some talking.... Faster'n I could pull the trigger he laid this quirt of his across my eyes and blinded me. I threw a couple of shots blind, couldn't see a thing, Sherry. ... He knocked me down and I reckon they all put the boots to me. Well, soon as I could travel I came on here. He's in town, Sherry, but he's leaving tomorrow, west with the wagon train. His name is—"

"Cord Macklin," Sherrill said tightly. "I met him this afternoon. I knew I was going to have to kill him sometime. But I didn't know just why—then."

"That's him," Patchin affirmed. "Koogle and Spicer, the other two, are with him. Sherry, I'd give anything if I could have my eyes back just long enough, just an hour or so. But it's no use.... You'll take care of it for me, Sherry?"

"I'll take care of it, Patch," Sherrill said softly. "I'll take care of everything."

Patchin smiled under the bandage. "I knew you would, boy."

"I'm going to get you a nice room in the hotel," Sherrill told him. "Get you some good food and a doctor. You'll be all right, Patch."

"Never mind about me," said Patchin. "You take care of that business. I'm all right here, Sherry. The lady brought me something to eat."

"Shut up!" Sherrill ordered roughly. "You're going to the hotel. If I don't come back myself I'll send somebody. Harry Connover's boys will treat you right. Rest easy now, Patch, and don't worry about a thing." Sherrill stood up and leaned forward to press Patchin's shoulder before turning toward the door where the girl was standing guard, the gun enormous and rather ridiculous in her dainty hand.

Nina Montez had to lead Sherrill out like a child then, for his own eyes were suddenly and scaldingly blinded.

CHAPTER FOUR

Harry Connover smiled behind his desk and waved Sherrill to a chair in the office at the rear of the Royal Saloon and gambling emporium. Harry was small and plump and neat, with a pale, soft face, cold hard eyes, and the usual thin cigar in his trimly mustached mouth. He was always suave and calmly controlled, a little man of vast experience and great assurance. Harry Connover regarded the world and its inhabitants with detached and ironical amusement as well as interest.

"Well, your friend Patchin is safely ensconced in the best available room at the Queen's Hotel," he announced in his cultured tone. "One of the finest physicians west of the Alleghenies is in attendance. No doubt purely through devotion to you, Nina Montez has volunteered to act as nurse, and as you well know, Nina can be very comforting to a man. But you, Sherry, look extremely worried, and likely with reason. I understand that Lavery has finally unleashed his dogs of war, and that you are not long for this vale of tears."

"That seems to be the general opinion," agreed Sherrill, reaching for one of the long, slender cigars in the hammered-silver humidor. "Lavery has my money; now he wants my life."

"Unfortunate that you didn't see fit to deposit your money at my tables," sighed Harry Connover. "But no matter. Your major mistake, of course, was Nina. You were safe until Lilli turned on you, son. Lavery adheres to a strange code in these affairs. He never has Lil's lovers executed until she herself calls for it. What are your plans, Sherry?"

"I don't know, Harry. I don't know what to do."

"Health dictates that you leave town, my boy. Why don't you go with the wagon train? The Romneys would welcome you, and the daughter is very lovely."

Sherrill's face hardened into a smooth mask. "Don't be a fool, Harry! Where would I fit in with a wagon train? I'd go crazy out there in the wilderness."

"You have something else in mind, Sherry. Something connected perhaps with Patchin's misfortune?"

"Yes," Sherrill said flatly. "I have some killing to do."

"I know what happened down the river," Connover told him. "But you can't kill those men *now*."

"You know everything," muttered Sherrill. "Why can't I?"

"Because it would leave the wagon train without leadership. Macklin is in charge; Spicer and Koogle are his lieutenants. Killing them would wreck the train before it started, Sherry. You wouldn't want to do that."

"They've got to die."

"I am in full agreement with that," assented Connover. "But there's no time limit. Why not go with the train and settle accounts once you get there?"

"The devil with the train," Sherrill said. "I don't want any part of it. Why are you so anxious to get me out of town, Harry?"

Harry Connover laughed and spread his plump hands in protest. "I'm not, Sherry, not at all. I'm very fond of you, I enjoy your company, I should miss you a great deal. I admire your courage, your skill with guns and girls, cards and dice. But I do not wish to see you die here in these streets without a chance. And you will, son, if you stay in Bedloe Landing. I'll stake you for the trip, and generously. I'll see that Patchin has the best of care and attention."

"I don't like the idea of being run out by that bunch, Harry."

"It's senseless to stay and fight the whole pack—Mitchum, Holway, Dakin, and all the rest. It's suicide, Sherry. As good as you are, my boy, you aren't bulletproof. Go with the wagons, go with the Romneys."

"I don't belong with people like the Romneys," Sherrill said with some bitterness.

"Why not?" countered Connover. "You're a gentleman—or will be when you stop running wild and start growing up. I know your family name, son. Even if I didn't I could tell there's blood and breeding behind you. The Romneys represent the better stock of New England, but you are more aristocratic than that. You are—"

Sherrill gestured sharply. "That's all dead."

Connover shook his balding head with a smile. "That never dies, Sherry. But getting back to the point in question: As I see it, there is only one course for you: to help the train through safely and then deal with Macklin and the others."

"I can't see any wagon train for me, Harry. Sorry, but I can't."

Connover leaned forward across the desk, his face grave. "They say our friend Lavery is *betting* that this train won't get through." He made the statement with cold, quiet emphasis.

Sherrill straightened, stared incredulously, and swore softly. "A heck of a thing to bet on. I should've killed him last night."

Connover poured two drinks from a cut-glass decanter and they sipped them slowly in silence. Sherrill studied the blue smoke curling from his cigar. Connover held his glass to the light and twirled it with deliberate care. At last Connover spoke.

"Your guns would be a great help on the trail, Sherry."

For several minutes Sherrill was lost in contemplation. Then he drained his glass and looked at the man behind the desk. "I'll think it over, Harry."

"Keep out of sight," advised Connover, "or you'll be too busy dodging bullets to do much thinking. You need money, don't you?" He pushed some bills and a stack of silver dollars across the polished wood. "Don't let Lavery get this now, Sherry! There'll be considerable more if you accompany the train."

"Thanks, Harry." Sherrill stood up, smiling, feeling better with money in his pocket once more. "I'll be back to see you in a while."

"Don't go out the front way," warned Connover. "They'll be watching out there. Even you, Sherry, can't shoot more than two ways simultaneously. Go out this door, if you insist on going. I should send some of my boys with you."

"No, I think better alone," Sherrill said from the rear door.

It was full night when Sherrill stepped out into the alley. The sky glittered with stars, and the street noises came to him as he stood there breathing deeply in an attempt to clear the confusion of his head. He felt alone, bewildered and lost, a way that he was unaccustomed to feeling and did not approve at all. He should be striding toward the river to find Cord Macklin and those other two foul creatures who had driven Veronica to her death and blinded Patchin. In his hotel room, Patch would be waiting in endless dark for Sherrill to come and tell him that Macklin, Koogle and Spicer had paid with their lives.

But Connover was correct: Sherry couldn't kill them as long as hundreds of men, women and children depended upon their guidance. Patch would have to wait.... Meanwhile Sherrill's first duty was to keep himself alive, and the odds were high against that while he remained in Bedloe Landing. With an effort he banished the impulse to go get drunk and forget the whole business; to let Lavery's boys come, and blast a few of them before they got him.... No, he couldn't do that; he wasn't playing a single hand any more. Sherrill had more than his own life to preserve now. His eyes were Patch's eyes, and his guns were Patch's. Connover had mentioned something about growing up. It was time Sherry started.

The alley was black, and before his eyes were completely adjusted to it someone came running into him, a woman, and he recognized Lilli Lavery's perfume as he let his right-hand gun drop back into its sheath, his left arm going around her full-blown figure. "Don't shoot, Lilli," he laughed. "You almost got me this afternoon." She ceased gasping and struggling at the sound of his voice and leaned against him with a sigh.

"Oh, Sherry, thank goodness I'm in time! You can't go out this way, Sherry; they're waiting to kill you. I had to come and tell you."

"I thought you wanted me killed, Lilli."

"No, no, don't be a fool!" cried Lilli Lavery. "I was out of my head this afternoon, crazy with jealousy. You know I love you, Sherry."

Sherrill grinned. 'I had my doubts when that bullet clipped my ear."

"Please, darling, this is serious," she beseeches. "My husband has sent them to shoot you. Come with me, out the other way. I'll take you where you'll be safe, where no one will bother us." Lilli was shoving him frantically toward the opposite end of the alley.

"You might be leading me into a trap," he said jestingly.

She shook his arm furiously. "Don't say that! I'll shoot you myself if you talk that way!"

"See? You're more dangerous than Mitch and the boys."

Lilli laughed and pressed close to him. "In a different way, darling, a much nicer way. Come on, Sherry. My carriage is waiting in the back street."

"Where are we going?" he asked with real concern.

"The only place in town where you'll be safe, where nobody can touch you. Nobody but me, Sherry. Darling, that Nina is nothing to you, is she? I should've known .... And that little farm girl with the wagon train? They say she is very beautiful. You've only seen her once? That is good; that's enough. I'm the woman for you, Sherry. You and I—"

Sherrill was thinking rapidly as she chattered on and on. Probably her house *was* the safest place in town for him. Jay Lavery never went there, and his men had strict orders to keep away. No one went there unless expressly invited by Lilli herself.

There were the richest foods, the finest liquors, an excellent colored cook, and an unobtrusive Creole maid. He was far from anxious for. Lilli's company, but if she was on the level that actually would be the best spot to spend the evening. If she wasn't— well, the fireworks might as well begin now as any other time. Sherrill was getting that old reckless urge for action.

"To your house?" he asked.

"Where else?" laughed Lilli. "Come on, my darling."

As they stepped into the quiet back street vagrant lamplight touched the woman's head with gleaming gold. The vehicle waiting in the shadows was really an elegant closed coach with a Negro driver and two horses. Lilli believed in doing everything in style. He was helping her in ahead of him when her sudden scream split the night.

Sherrill was already dodging back and drawing as a blinding explosion seared his cheek. His boot-heel caught on the uneven boards of the walk and he fell backward as flame leaped at him again from the carriage. Flat on his back, Sherrill fired at the white-sleeved arm that must belong to Jay Lavery and saw the arm jerk back. The coach hurtled forward after the frightened plunging horses. Dust billowed up in the murky light as the rig careened wildly down the street into darkness.

Rolling over swiftly, Sherrill threw himself headlong into the shelter of the alleyway as bullets beat the dirt about him and ricocheted off the brick walls. When the firing ceased, Sherrill crouched across the alley and crept back toward its mouth, keeping low and tight against the wall. At first glance the street seemed empty, but there were furtive movements in the shadows across the way. Patiently Sherrill waited for a target.

A gun crashed and gravel showered Sherrill as he fired back at the muzzle-blast; he heard a man grunt and curse in pain as he fell threshing into the weeds of the vacant lot over there. Two more livid streaks stabbed the dimness from another angle and lead scored the stone near Sherry's brow. He emptied his right-hand gun in that direction and heard the scuffing thud of running boots. The wounded man in the weeds was crawling away in the darkness, sobbing and moaning, cursing the others for leaving him.

Sherrill reloaded while he had the chance. He thought they had all gone when a shot roared out from in front of the abandoned Blue Bird Opera House, and Sherrill glimpsed Dakin's shark-face as the man ducked forward into the inadequate shelter of a solitary darkened lamppost. That danged idiot was always taking chances, trying to prove himself the equal of Holway and Mitchum.

Coldly Sherrill brought his .44 to bear upon that post and opened up. Dakin's hands flew out as the slugs staggered him off sideways. Teetering forward, Dakin groped in desperation for the pole, but it was out of reach. Lurching from side to side, still straining as if that post meant salvation, his shark-teeth bared, Dakin toppled slowly face first into the gutter.

The others were coming back now. Bullets ripped the wooden walk, kicked up dirt, and screeched off the bricks above Sherrill's head, spraying him with stonedust. Sherry triggered until the Colt was empty again, aiming at the flitting forms behind the muzzle flashes, drawing back as the lead whined closer. There were too many of them. Turning finally, Sherrill ran for the back door of the Royal, reaching it just as black figures blurred the other end of the passage.

Harry Connover let him in and locked the door, smiling at his powder-stained face and the smoking gun in his big hand. "You didn't stay long, son."

Sherrill grinned. "No, Harry. It's kind of hot and noisy out there. Reckon I'll hang in here, if you don't mind. It's more peaceful."

"There *was* a lot of racket," confessed Connover. "Anybody get hurt?"

"Couple of fellows," drawled Sherrill. "One serious—the Shark."

"The community will miss that lovable character," Connover said. "Well, Sherry, the game is wide open now. You'll have to leave the Landing if you want to live. And you shouldn't wear that red shirt, son. It makes too good a target."

Sherrill laughed softly. "Maybe that's why Lilli gave it to me."

CHAPTER FIVE

After two hours alone with his thoughts and Connover's cigars and whiskey, Sherrill had made little progress and was beginning to get restless and fretful. He was not in the habit of sitting back to think things out; he always had obeyed the impulse of the moment and the devil with the consequences. But that wouldn't do this time. There were too many people involved, too many angles to consider. Try as he would, Sherrill could not straighten them out into any satisfactory pattern.

Once, upon hearing Patchin's story, he would have gone directly after Macklin and his two subordinates. Now there were the Romneys and all those other hundreds of the wagon train to think about. Harry's suggestion about going with the train was the sensible solution, but Sherrill did not want to go. The thought of that long, tedious, uncomfortable journey across the barren wastes oppressed him. He lacked the patience to endure the endless monotony, the slow plodding through sand and heat, the emptiness of prairie and forest. He was too fond of lights and laughter and music, the smiles of women, the gay fellowship of saloons, the excitement of the gaming tables. He was selfish and he was soft.

On the other hand, he either had to leave Bedloe Landing or fight it out with Lavery's crew, and to go against the whole gang, as Harry said, was suicidal. He wondered if Lilli had lured him into that trap outside, or if Lavery had posted his men and slipped into the carriage unbeknown to her. Her scream had sounded spontaneous and genuine enough.... But who could tell about a woman like Lilli?

It didn't matter much either way. Lilli was the real power behind the Lavery gambling dynasty, with Jay more or less a figurehead. If Jay was betting that the train would not get through, it was on Lil's instigation. Anger started its slow red swirl in Sherrill at this thought. Anyone who would wager on the lives of hundreds of emigrant families didn't deserve to live any more than Cord Macklin did.

Then the vision of Molly Romney returned to still his anger and obscure his thinking. There was a woman, a thoroughbred, with style and class in every line and movement. For a girl like that a man could give up a lot. Even his freedom, perhaps.... But Sherrill wasn't yet ready to yield that. It wouldn't be fair to the woman, either, after the madcap, roistering, philandering life he had known. He stood up, yawning and stretching, as Harry Connover came back into his private office. Sherrill asked him what was happening out front.

"Nothing of importance—as yet," replied Connover. "Some of Lavery's hired hands tried to get in, but my boys told them the Royal was out of bounds tonight. Dakin is dead, as you inferred, and Sheriff Slocumb has a warrant out for you. Another valid reason why you should go west, young man. The emigrants are up in arms about something, I hear, but the details to date are vague. Some girl seems to have disappeared from camp, and they fear she will be pressed into a life of sin in the River Belle or some other Bedloe institution of ill fame. What's the matter, Sherry; aren't you comfortable here?"

"No," said Sherrill. "I appreciate your hospitality, but I'm afraid it's wasted on me. I can't think any more—beyond cards and women."

"Well, you have been trying to, at least. That is encouraging. Have you arrived at any decision whatsoever?"

Sherrill shook his head miserably. "Not yet, Harry."

Connover examined his well kept hands. "The fireworks out back should have convinced you that the Landing is certain to be unhealthy for you from now on."

"I know. But I still can't picture myself pioneering."

There came a rapping on the door. Connover opened it and the Romney brothers stood there, strangely stern and stiff. Connover beckoned them inside. Sherrill's welcoming smile faded as he saw their faces. Whit was drawn bleak and pale under the tan; Jud was smolderingly dark and ugly. Both wore gun belts and carried carbines; both were tense and stark.

"Molly's gone," Whit said, hoarse and strained. "Somebody's got Molly."

Sherrill felt chilled in the pit of the stomach, and the cold prickled up his spine and tightened his scalp. His heart hammered in the hollowness of his chest, while he was icy cold all over. "Where's Macklin?" he asked, his voice sounding odd in his own ears.

"Getting the men ready to march on the town," Jud said. "They figure it's Lavery."

Sherrill could think now. In this crisis his brain raced sharp and clear and sure.

"It may be Lavery," he said through his teeth. "But they don't want to leave that camp unguarded tonight. They might find their wagons on fire and their horses gone. Harry, send somebody down there on the run. At least half of them should stay in camp and be ready for anything."

"But why?" asked Whit in shocked surprise. "Why should anybody attack us, Sherry? We've done nothing here...."

"Never mind now," Sherrill told him.

Harry Connover was at the door. "I'll send three or four of the boys to organize a guard over the camp." He went out quickly.

"Right now it's Molly we want to find," Jud choked out.

"We'll find her," Sherrill said with quiet grimness. "If we have to tear this town apart, we'll find her!" Pulling off his scarlet shirt,

Sherrill snatched a short buckskin jacket off the wall and slipped swiftly into it. Connover re-entered the room and regarded him with approval.

"There, you look better, Sherry. My boys are off to the river, so the camp will be safe. Have you any ideas, son?"

"I have a strong hunch," said Sherrill, remembering Lilli Lavery's reference to the little farm girl with the wagon train.

"Cord Macklin thinks they've got Molly in the River Belle," Judson said.

"Let 'em go there then," said Sherrill. "The more of Lavery's men they tie up the better. Did you bring horses?"

"Yes, and we brought an extra one for you, Sherry," Whitmore said, eager now, gaining confidence from Sherrill.

"Good," Sherrill replied. "That'll save time and trouble."

"Don't forget, Sherry," warned Connover. "They'll shoot you on sight."

Sherrill grinned. "They'll have to shoot right fast. Come on, boys."

"Watch out for Slocumb and his men, too."

"They'd better watch out for us," Sherrill said. "Let's go."

They went striding out through the close-packed, smoke-veiled saloon, and a suddenly silent crowd opened a way for them to the swing-doors, men and women turning to watch the three tall boys with the hard-set faces. *"Sherry and the Romneys!"* ran the hushed word. *"Brothers of that girl. Trouble's goin' to break loose somewhere tonight!"* They went out front with eyes alert and hands ready. The three horses were at the rack, and they mounted quickly and wheeled away.

Lavery's gunmen had apparently been called back to the River Belle, but Sheriff Slocumb, with Vasoll and two other deputies, sighted Sherrill and came shouting across the street to head off the riders. Sherry drove his horse straight at them, with the Romneys hard after him, and the sheriff's party scattered wildly before the flying hoofs. Guns exploded, bullets breathed close in the pale lamplight, and Sherrill saw the terror on Slocumb's fat face as the horse struck him and sent his gross bulk tumbling into the shadows. Vasoll, prone in the ditch, was firing furiously until Sherry's snap shot spouted dirt into his face. Sherrill rounded the corner on the gallop, the Romneys pounding in his wake. Letting the horses run, they left the square behind.

Glancing back over his shoulder, Sherry saw a growing crowd darken the plaza in front of the River Belle and judged that Cord Macklin and his pioneers must be closing in. Jay Lavery meant to win that bet, all right. Sherrill had no doubt that one motive behind the taking of Molly was to draw the emigrants away from camp. He was angered anew as he thought of the simple honest families with the wagon train, the women and children of all ages. There were two types of gambler: Lavery was one, Connover the other. They had nothing in common but their occupation.

Sherrill settled down to ride, hitting a fast pace, twisting from street to street to throw off a pursuit that he didn't really expect. That demonstration in front of the River Belle was likely to keep Slocumb and his deputies busy for some time. It would also require the full attention of Mitchum, Holway, and the rest of Lavery's personal bodyguards.... Sherrill found it good to be in the saddle again, and he was enjoying his night ride. Sometimes it seemed that action was the only thing that truly satisfied him.

Nearing the home of Lilli Lavery, they slowed the horses to a walk. By night, the trim adobe structure looked much the same as the other houses on the street, with only a hint of elegance in lamplight glowing through rich brocaded curtains. But Sherrill was familiar with the interior, which Lilli had filled with extravagantly luxurious furnishings.

They left the horses in the back alley through which Sherrill had fled that afternoon. Sherry still had a key to the front door, and he handed it to Jud with instructions to move in that way after they had made entrance from the rear. Sherrill and Whit crossed the back yard as Jud slid silently away toward the front.

The house had a serene, homelike aspect in the quiet night. Obviously neither Sherrill nor the emigrants were expected here.

Carefully they climbed over the rail at the end of the porch and crept toward the kitchen door. It was impossible to see inside through the draped windows. There might be a reception committee, after all. Sherrill drew his right-hand gun and Whit followed suit. The back door opened abruptly and a man loomed darkly in the aperture. Sherry and Whit halted outside the radius of light. The sentry stepped out to peer around. Sherrill leaped forward just as the fellow spotted them. The man's hand jerked downward, but Sherry's gun barrel slashed across his skull, dropping him heavily to the boards.

"Get his gun, Whit," Sherrill said, striding over the body and into the kitchen. Whit Romney stooped to lift the gun from the unconscious man's holster and entered on Sherrill's heels.

A man named Wilkins was starting up from his chair, revolver half drawn, when he saw Sherrill. Gaping into the muzzle of Sherry's .44, Wilkins wagged his head and sank back into the chair, raising his hands head-high with a sheepish grin. He knew Sherrill and he knew when he was licked. The blond boy with Sherry also handled those two irons in an efficient manner.

"Where is she, Wilkins?" demanded Sherrill, taking the man's gun.

Wilkins stared stupidly. "Who, uh, Miss Lilli? Why, she's out front somewhere. She—"

"Who's with her?" Sherry shot at him sharply.

"Why, uh, nobody," mumbled Wilkins. "Nobody I know of, Sherry."

Sherrill laughed. "*You* wouldn't be here if she was alone. I didn't suppose she let any of her husband's gorillas in here, Call her out."

"Miss Lilli!" Wilkins called plaintively. "Come on out here, Miss Lilli, please."

She came clicking and swishing along the corridor into the kitchen, her formal tentative smile freezing and vanishing as she saw Sherrill and Whit with guns in hand. Her bleached blonde head sagged slightly, her chin dropped, and her handsome face slacked into tired lines. But her recovery was rapid and remarkable, her violet eyes lighting and the smile flashing brilliantly once more.

"Oh, Sherry! Thank heaven you are all right! Sherry, I didn't know *he* was in the carriage tonight. Please believe me, darling, I didn't know." She gestured in helpless appeal.

"Never mind that," said Sherrill. "Where's Molly Romney?"

Lilli went on as if she hadn't heard. "I'm getting rid of Lavery. He went too far tonight, Sherry, and I'm sending him away. The River Belle is mine anyway. Will you run it for me, Sherry?"

"Where is Molly Romney?" he asked slowly and distinctly.

Lilli Lavery hesitated, the smile dimming and the violet eyes blinking. "Oh, the little farm girl, you mean? Why, she's here; she's safe," Lilli said finally, soothingly. "I knew you'd be after her sooner or later. My husband, he gets crazier all the time. Taking a girl like that from her family!" She shook her golden head sadly. "I don't know what Jay was thinking of. I'll get her for you, Sherry." She was the gracious hostess now.

"I'll go with you," Sherrill said. "Not that I mistrust you, Lilli.... Whit, you keep an eye on these two."

He walked after her along the corridor, scanning the familiar setting as Lilli bent to unlock a door. "For her own protection, Sherry," she explained, "I locked her in this room. Such a lovely girl, too."

Molly Romney walked out, straight and calm and easy, directly into Sherrill's arms. There was no sign of panic or hysteria in her. She smiled and stepped back to look up at Sherrill. Her face was clear, her gray eyes dry and serene. She said: "I thought you'd come, Sherry. Are my brothers with you?"

Sherrill nodded. "Looks like you're all right, Molly."

"Yes, I'm all right. Mrs. Lavery was very kind. I hope the folks didn't take it too hard, though."

Lilli was watching them narrowly, dangerous sparks in her strange violet eyes, her slim white hands twitching nervously, her red lips writhing with emotion. Sherrill spoke to her over Molly's dark head.

"Don't pull that toy pistol again, Lilli. I'll kill you if you do." There was absolutely no expression in his voice.

Lilli spread her palms theatrically and tragically in the vague golden lamplight. "I give you up, Sherry. I let you go, with my blessing."

"Thank you," Sherrill said with mild satire. "Lead the way, Lil."

"One minute, please," cut in a cool, superior voice, and Jay Lavery was in the hallway behind them, his right arm in a sling, his left hand holding a derringer firmly on Sherrill. "If there's killing to be done, I believe it is my turn." He was immaculate as usual, even with the wounded arm and battered face, a tall dapper figure with an air of lofty disdain.

Sherrill had pushed Molly aside as he turned to the front of the house to face Lavery, regretting that he had holstered his six-gun on seeing the girl. Lilli had moved out of line and was watching with a poker face.

"Well, well," Sherrill drawled. "How long since this house has been open to you, Lavery?"

"Very humorous," said Jay Lavery. "You're a great wit, Sherrill. I imagine you think you have made a fool and a laughing stock of me this last month. Possibly you have, in certain quarters. But I have always taken my satisfaction in laughing last, Sherrill. I shall be laughing when you die here on Lilli's polished floor."

"You'd better think it over, Lavery." Sherrill was stalling desperately for time. Whit didn't know what was going on here and couldn't leave the kitchen anyway, but where the devil was

Judson? "This place is surrounded. If I die here you'll hang before I'm cold, Lavery."

Jay laughed a brittle laugh. "I don't care what happens to me, Sherrill, as long as I see you die. Are you going to reach or just stand and take it?"

"There's somebody behind you now, Lavery."

"That's an old one," Lavery sneered. "Are you ready?" He lifted the derringer with a flourish.

The weapon had just come level with Sherrill's breast when there *was* someone behind Jay Lavery. It was Jud Romney, gliding in fast from the front door, six-gun in hand. Lavery sensed danger and started to whirl, even before Lilli screamed, but Jud was already on top of him, clubbing his gun barrel savagely down upon Lavery's pomaded head. Lavery's knees folded and he crumpled at once under that crushing blow, falling limp and loose without a sound. In the pale yellow light Sherrill saw that Lavery's eyes were wide open, bulging and staring sightlessly. The River Belle belonged to Lilli now all right, whether or not it had before. She was the sole owner.

Molly Romney had turned away, her face to the wall, but Lilli was gazing at the lifeless form on the floor.

"Just in time, Judson," Sherrill said. "Let's get out of here now."

"Guess I hit him too hard," muttered Jud, stepping across Lavery and past Sherrill. "Molly! Are you all right?" He caught his sister to him, holding her hard, and they moved slowly toward the kitchen together. Whit's voice rising happily as he saw them.

Still staring at her husband's body, Lilli shook her blonde head and laughed queerly. "Now you can stay in Bedloe Landing, Sherry. He was nothing anyway. I'm better off without him. You will be my partner, Sherry. We'll run the Landing, in time the whole Mississippi. Can't you see, darling? ..."

Sherrill looked at her and turned his head from side to side.

"All right, you fool!" flared Lilli Lavery. "Go with your little farm girl. But I'll tell you one thing: that wagon train will never get across the plains!" Her voice rose to an insane pitch. "And that wench's hair will make a rare trophy in some Apache wigwam! Although I understand they prefer blondes."

Sherrill's hand flicked out automatically, the palm smacking loudly against the woman's painted cheek. Recoiling to the wall, Lilli hung there, shaken and panting like an animal, her scarlet mouth working. With one last withering look Sherrill left her there, quivering and gasping, and walked back to the kitchen.

"Let's go," he said brusquely, herding the Romneys to the door. "Wilkins, the house is yours."

The sentry on the back veranda was still unconscious or pretending to be. They helped Molly to the ground. In the dark alley Sherrill lifted her into his saddle and walked beside her to the street.

"You can ride with me, Sherry," the girl said.

"No, I'll walk in." Sherrill wanted to go with them, but the feeling returned that he did not belong with such fine people, that he was somehow tainted and unworthy. Everything in him yearned to accompany Molly Romney, but he forced the desire down, blotted it out with bitter remorse. She was not for him, or anyone like him. It simply wasn't meant to be.

"Come on up behind me, Sherry," invited Whit.

"No, I'd rather walk."

"Sherry, you've got to come with us," Jud said.

"You folks ride for home," Sherrill insisted, slapping the flank of Molly's horse to start them moving.

Perplexed and troubled, they cantered away in the faint light and ragged shadows. A short space off they reined up and turned back with a single accord. Clenching his hands and teeth until they ached, swallowing the painful lump in his throat, Sherrill steeled himself for what he had to do.

"Keep going, hang you!" he yelled. "I got a date!"

The clop of hoofs echoed back in the night as they rode on, bewildered and sorrowful. Smiling a wry smile, Sherrill started walking in the same direction.

Well, that was the end of that. He had killed it with one cruel, relentless stroke. It was the most merciful way, after all. Recalling the feeling of Molly in his arms, he shivered deep inside. But there was no use thinking about it: he would never hold her again.

Sherrill had grimmer tasks at hand, a mission to perform for his old pardner, Patchin. In his present state of grief and loss and frustration, Sherrill decided that he might as well get it over with. The wagon train would be just as well off without those three vultures, perhaps a lot better. In a hard hating mood, the blood lust up, Sherrill looked forward to the encounter. His lips thinned against his teeth as he lengthened his stride toward town and caressed the gun-handles on his hips.

CHAPTER SIX

The square was solidly filled with surging humanity when Sherrill got there. To see over the massed bobbing heads, men were perched on barrels, boxes, hitch-racks, wooden awnings, wagons, and rooftops, and people of both sexes were leaning from second-story windows around the plaza. Evidently Sheriff Slocumb and his deputies had found the situation too much to cope with, for they were nowhere in view. Practically everybody else in Bedloe Landing seemed to be present.

No one paid any attention to Sherrill, and he found it a pleasant relief to pass unnoticed for once. Nice to be in the audience for a change, instead of on the stage. But there was an electric tension in the air that signified danger. As Sherrill worked his way through the close-pressed bodies, he realized it wouldn't take much to ignite the powder here. One tiny spark would blow everything wide open.

The center of attraction was the facade of the River Belle. There were three entrances, and Lavery's gun-sharps were strung across in front of them, backed by some white-aproned bartenders with sawed-off shotguns. Holway strutted back and forth spitting tobacco juice, head thrusting arrogantly on the bull-neck, tough scarred face shining in a damp snarl under the lights, broad chest swelling, thumbs hooked into gun belt. Mitchum stood quiet and impassive, gaunt face solemn and sour, brooding like a lank country parson over an unruly congregation.

Sherrill wondered how they would react if they knew that Jay Lavery was lying dead out there in his wife's house. Chances were it wouldn't change them a bit. They probably knew that Lilli was the real boss, and Lilli was still very much alive.

Big Cord Macklin, quirt on wrist, headed the rifle-bearing pioneers, flanked by a large pompous man and a thin ferret-faced fellow, Koogle and Spicer beyond a doubt. At the sight of them Sherrill went tight and hot all over, throat constricted, mouth dry, hands distended clawlike over his gun butts. But Mr. Romney was with them, dependent on them. Mr. Romney, Ed Deal, Wilson, Potter, and other good men.... With a sigh Sherrill relaxed and let the fire die out in him. This was neither the time nor the place.

Squirming through the jammed mob, Sherrill was trying to figure a way to break this up before some flare-up precipitated a wholesale slaughter. Holway had stopped pacing now and stood near Mitchum by the central doorway. They were the key men, of course. If he could get them covered and announce that Molly Romney had been found, there would be no shooting. It was impossible to get through to the front rank of emigrants and tell them the girl was safe. There was so much noise that shouting it from the outer fringes would be futile. Sherrill could see only one way to accomplish it, and that meant taking a long chance. But he had been taking those chances all his life.

With knees and hips, elbows and shoulders, Sherrill fought his way out of the jostling crowd and circled behind the large general store adjacent to Lavery's place. In the alley between the two buildings was a little-used side entrance to the River Belle. As Sherrill had hoped, there was nobody guarding this door. In fact, the interior was virtually deserted except for a lone bartender, because the customers had flocked out front to watch the show.

Drawing both guns, Sherrill slipped in through the batwing doors. The bartender's eyes widened in startled recognition, and he quickly raised his hands shoulder-high, fingers spread as if to emphasize their emptiness.

"Keep 'em there," Sherrill said. "I'm not gunning for anybody. I just want to break that up out there."

The man nodded almost eagerly. "Don't worry about me, Sherry. I ain't paid to handle no guns."

Sherrill went swiftly toward the central doorway, where a few men were clumped peeping over the swing-doors. A fat barkeeper with a sawed-off shotgun saw Sherrill coming, and all three chins dropped on his chest as his mouth gaped wide. He started to drop the shotgun, but Sherrill shook his head.

"Hang onto it, chief. We're going out front. One side, please, boys."

The others moved aside in astonishment. Sherrill prodded the fat man through the batwings and followed closely, hidden from the front by that immense bulk. Holway and Mitchum were still side by side, eyes on the riflemen from the wagon train. Sherrill slid behind them and jabbed a gun barrel into each of their backs.

"All right, boys," he said clearly. "Reach high and tell your friends not to try any tricks. The party's over. The Romney girl has been found."

Mitchum and Holway elevated their hands deliberately, twisting their heads to stare in surprise and disgust at Sherrill. He lifted his voice. "Mr. Romney! Your daughter is safe back in camp with Whit and Jud."

"How do *you* know?" sneered Cord Macklin, flicking his quirt.

For an instant Sherrill all but forgot Holway and Mitchum in the burning need to turn his guns loose on Macklin and the other two. Then sanity returned. "Shut up and get back to your wagons," he advised, "before somebody gets hurt here."

"Ain't you the cute one though?" Holway said. "Regular little jack-in-the-box!"

"Tell your playmates to get inside, Mitch," said Sherrill. "Way inside. Way back to the bar."

Mitchum did so in sad, sonorous tones. The white aprons and sawed-off shotguns vanished, and the rest of Lavery's hands drifted after them as the mob began to disperse.

Mitchum turned his long, mournful face. "Told 'em she wasn't here, Sherry. Stubborn, these people." He yawned and slouched indifferently toward the swing-doors. "Seems to be all settled now. Let's adjourn to the bar, Holly."

Holway lingered to eye Sherrill with bold insolence. "You changed your shirt, pretty boy. You look prettier in that red one."

"Thanks," smiled Sherrill. "I'll wear it for you again sometime. Get along inside, Holway."

"Talk big," muttered Holway, shouldering the doors in rage, "while you can still talk!"

Sherrill moved quickly out into the milling throng and crossed toward the Royal, still absentmindedly carrying his guns in hand. The men of the wagon train were trailing off toward camp behind Cord Macklin and his assistants, but Mr. Romney hung back to follow Sherrill across the square, his Sharps rifle ready and covering Sherry every foot of the way, his tired brown eyes ranging to all sides.

Sheriff Slocumb, Vasoll and another deputy, appearing now that the crisis had passed and the mob was breaking up, cut across to intercept Sherrill in front of the Royal. The sheriff was limping badly and his deputies were plainly reluctant.

"I got a warrant for you, Sherrill," wheezed Slocumb. "You better come along peaceable like."

"Save it for tomorrow," Sherrill said wearily. "Don't try to take me tonight." He went on past them as if they did not exist.

Glaring after him, Vasoll swore and reached for his holster, with the sudden idea of becoming a local hero by drilling the notorious Sherrill, even if it were in the back.

Mr. Romney brought the Sharps up and spoke distinctly. "I wouldn't try that if I was you, sonny."

Vasoll looked at Mr. Romney's rifle, changing his mind abruptly. Slocumb started to reprimand Romney for interfering with the law, when Sherrill spun around with the two Colts leveled.

"I told you tomorrow," Sherrill said, waving them impatiently away with the left-hand gun.

Slocumb and his aides were already fading into the darkness. Slocumb said: "Tomorrow Bedloe Landin's goin' to see a hangin', friend."

Sherrill laughed. "In that case I might as well shoot the sheriff and a few deputies." The departing boots quickened perceptibly as the sheriff's delegation left the plaza. Sherrill turned to the stocky man with the rifle. "Thank you, Mr. Romney. Will you join me in a drink?"

"Like to, Sherry, but I should be getting back to the family. My wife was pretty upset, of course. We owe you a lot for finding Molly so soon for us. … I wish you'd come along with us tomorrow, boy. You're more than welcome, Sherry. And there's nothing for you here but trouble."

Sherrill smiled and shook his head. "I sure appreciate it, Mr. Romney. But I reckon I'll get drunk instead."

"Helps a man sometimes," admitted Mr. Romney. "Temporarily, at least. But you've got to be careful, Sherry."

"I will be," promised Sherrill, sheathing his guns at last. "I'm safe in the Royal."

"Molly was all right?"

"Perfectly," Sherrill assured him. "The best of luck to you and your family."

They shook hands firmly and warmly. Mr. Romney turned down Front Street toward the river flats, and Sherrill watched him go. Then he lifted his gaze to the lighted windows that marked Patchin's room in the Queen's Hotel and shook his head in weary indecision. He burned to take Patch's revenge on Macklin and the other two, yet he did not wish to handicap and imperil the wagon train. Perhaps a few drinks would help indicate one definite course or other. Once his mind was set, he would go to see Patchin.

Men made a space for Sherrill at the busy bar, and a barkeeper set up a bottle and glass. "On the house, Sherry." He noticed that Fiddle Filchock, the Indian scout, was very drunk at a corner table, his shaggy head drooping over his greasy buckskin arms on the wood. Well, Fiddle would have plenty of time to sober up before they got into Indian territory.... Along the bar they were still discussing Sherrill's performance across the square. "...They're s'posed to be huntin' Sherry high an' low, see? An' hanged if he don't pop up outa nowhere an' lay his irons on Mitchum an' Holway. I'll never forget the look on them two when they saw Sherry...."

A dozen men wanted to buy Sherrill drinks, but he declined with quiet courtesy. His own bottle was lowered several inches when a Connover employee called him and pointed to the office door. As he refilled his glass, Sherrill observed that Fiddle Filchock had passed out completely and was snoring in the corner. Smiling and nodding absently to the men and women who greeted him, Sherrill carried his glass back to the office.

Harry Connover sat at his desk, smiling faintly and toying with a liquor glass and the usual thin cigar. Sherrill closed the door and crossed the room to stand before him.

"Did they hit the wagon train, Harry?" he asked.

"They started an attack but it didn't last long," Connover said. "They were driven off immediately. Did you have any trouble getting the girl, Sherry?"

"Not much. But Jay Lavery managed to get himself killed."

"So?" Connover registered considerable surprise for him. "A good thing. But Lilli will carry on; nothing will change much. Have you decided on anything yet?"

"Can't seem to make up my mind, Harry," confessed Sherrill.

Connover made an odd gesture with his glass. At that moment Sherrill sensed another presence in the room, someone lurking behind him. He pivoted smoothly, whiskey slopping over his left hand as he drew with his right. The gun was halfway out when something smashed his head with stunning force. Sherrill bowed under the impact, his knees struck the floor, and he swayed there watching his glass roll away unbroken, leaving an erratic trail of liquid on the boards. "Safe," he sighed in disgust, trying to raise his head that reeled heavily with blinding lights, thinking that even Harry had turned on him now. *"Safe!"*

He was still struggling to rise, fighting the nausea in his stomach and the weakness in his limbs, numb fingers dragging at the gun handle. Suddenly the flashing lights accelerated into a sickening swirl, flared high and then faded into a swift blackout. Sherrill fell face forward and never felt the wood beneath him.

CHAPTER SEVEN

Ages later Sherrill awoke to agony and a strange swaying, jolting sensation that he could not identify. It seemed a continuation of the long fearful nightmare he had been caught in. His aching eyes opened, dry and grained, to the sun-bright canvas overhead, a pain stabbed through his eyeballs into the heated haze of his brain. Mouth and throat were parched, his tongue swollen enormously, and fever consumed him as he lay sweating and ill in a smothering furnace, his body wrenched and wracked by that peculiar rocking, bumping motion. "Christopher," groaned Sherrill. "I never had a hangover like this before!" Then he remembered that shocking blow on the skull in Connover's office, and all at once he realized where he must be.

With a great effort he pushed himself partly upright and looked around at the jumble of bales, boxes, barrels, stacked furniture, household goods, piled blankets and clothing. Yes, it was the interior of a loaded wagon. He was with the wagon train, after all.... Fury blazed in him and he felt instinctively for his guns, but they were gone. Moaning and choking with thirst, Sherrill groped for the canteen that rested nearby, unscrewed the cap with thick fumbling fingers, and gulped greedily of the brackish water. Relieved somewhat but too weak to move, he lay back on the blankets and gave himself up to the ponderous lurching roll of the wagon.

For an interminable time Sherrill sprawled helplessly there on the rough bundles that constituted his crude bed, drenched with sweat and panting for breath, vaguely aware of outside noises and life. Slow rattling wheels, the creaking of wood and leather, the sounds of horses and men, cattle lowing plaintively, babies crying somewhere, the barking of dogs and shouting of children, whips cracking and a man cursing, the grinding scream of tortured axles, voices murmuring, draft animals snorting, and the laughter of women.

Rousing himself painfully to reach for another drink, he moaned at the rocketing agony in his head and damned forever the perfidy of Harry Connover. A feeling of loss and futile frustration tormented him until his pulsating eyes smarted on the verge of tears. As he set the canteen down, a paper crinkled in his jacket pocket. Fishing it out, Sherrill tried to focus his blurred vision on the neatly penned script. A message from his friend and betrayer:

> *Sorry, Sherry, but it seemed the only solution. I feared that you might have decided to do that job for Patchin and let the wagon train go to its uncertain, and no doubt unhappy, fate. You may not care for pioneering, my boy, but at the worst it is preferable to Slocumb's jail or a Bedloe Landing grave.*
>
> *You will find your guns, adequate money, supplies and equipment with the Romneys, even to horse and saddle and a new Henry repeating rifle. The red shirt also, but I do not recommend wearing it on the plains, as it might appeal to some young Indian brave. I am relying on you, son, to see that train safely through.*
>
> *The late Mr. Jay Lavery—you are now wanted for two killings—had wagered a fortune that the train will never reach Fort Bridger. Lilli, I believe, is even more avaricious than her ex-mate, and will certainly strive her utmost to collect that bet. You must be constantly on the alert, Sherry, and trust nobody outside of the Romneys. And even they appear to have a deluded faith in Macklin that*

may complicate matters. You will have trouble, but you thrive on that.

I truly feel that this trip is going to mark an important turning point in your life; that you will really grow up in the great West, and sometime thank me for what I had to do to get you on the train. The method was deplorably crude, I confess, but there was no time for delicacy.

I have explained everything to Patchin and he is in full agreement that this plan is best. He will get the finest of care, Sherry, and the doctor declares there is some chance of restoring his sight, at least in one eye.

A very great deal depends on you, my boy, more than you can possibly comprehend. Those people need you, Sherry; all those hundreds of men, women and children need you. Your guns will be dedicated to a better cause than ever before. Good luck, Sherry, until you return to your real reward—although I think you'll find your richest reward out there on the plains.

Your friend, please believe me,

Harry Connover.

P.S.—You mustn't construe my intentions as selfish, son, even if Lavery did talk me into covering some of his money.

Wearied from the exertion of reading, head throbbing fiercely and eyes watering, Sherrill sank back again into semi-consciousness in the stifling heat. The whole thing was ridiculous, a comic opera idea. He was a gunman, gambler, a ne'er-do-well, anything but a savior and guardian angel. Harry was either crazy or covering up on himself and his bet.... The sun beat down unmercifully on the scorched canvas as the wagon lumbered on. Sherrill's brain gyrated in ever-deepening spirals until at last, thankful for the release, he went all the way out once more.

He came reluctantly back to life to feel someone shaking him roughly, and looked up with glazed and crusted eyes at the dark glowering face of Cord Macklin. With a contemptuous grunt Macklin fastened both fists on Sherrill, jerking and heaving him upright. Sherrill was too weak and ill to stand, let alone offer any resistance. Snarling, Macklin dragged him bodily over bales and crates to the rear of the wagon. There was a tremendous bursting strength in the man, and Sherry was helpless as a child in his powerful clutches.

"Come on, you drunken dog!" Cord Macklin said. "No free riders on this train. Out you go!"

Macklin hurled Sherrill from the back end of the wagon to the red soil of the prairie and jumped down after him, ready to strike, but Sherrill's legs gave way, tumbling him awkwardly to the earth before Macklin could swing at him. Sherrill thrashed feebly around trying to get up, then flopped back and subsided, panting and moaning. The big man stood over him, that wicked quirt snaking from his wrist.

"Get up, you drunken hound!" snarled Macklin, prodding the inert form with the toe of his foot. "You ain't so almighty brave without them guns, are you? Get up on your hind legs like a man!" By that time Sherrill was beyond hearing or feeling, to say nothing of moving.

The long line of wagons had halted for a rest in the late afternoon, and a curious crowd gathered quickly, stolid bearded men, women with tired, sun-reddened faces, and wide-eyed children grateful for a break in the monotony. "Why, that's Sherry," said somebody. "The gun kid from Bedloe Landin'!"

"Yeah, that's him," Cord Macklin said in disgust. "Stowed away dead drunk in Ed Deal's wagon."

Ed Deal, fat and red-faced, whiskered and tobacco-stained, shook his shaggy graying head. "That boy ain't drunk, Cord. He's hurt and sick. Got a lump on his head bigger'n a pool ball."

"Well, he's no blasted good," said Macklin. "He's nobody we want on this train." His boot thudded into Sherrill's limp body, and the onlookers winced. "Get up or I'll give you a taste of that whip!" Cord Macklin's mouth was working strangely and his eyes shone black and wild as he snapped the quirt over that unconscious figure. He was ready to strike when hoofs drummed and the sudden shadow of a horseman loomed over him. Whit Romney, his fair face solemn and set, with a carbine crooked in his right arm.

"Hold on there, Cord," Whit said clearly. "That's a friend of mine."

Cord Macklin looked up, surprised and angered. "Friend or not, we ain't carryin' an' feedin' him. And you better not interfere, boy. I'm runnin' this outfit."

"You can run it," said Whit Romney, shifting the carbine. "But you're not touching him, Cord."

Macklin glared ferociously up at the boy on horseback, but Whit's gray eyes were as steady as the rifle he held under his right arm, finger on the trigger.

"You're gettin' too big for your britches, boy," Macklin growled. "I say we ain't carryin' free riders. I don't care whose friends they are."

"Nobody has to carry or feed Sherrill," said Whit evenly. "He's got all the equipment he needs and more supplies than most people."

"He has, huh?" Macklin was inwardly raging, but well aware of the quiet menace in this blond Romney boy and the general prestige of the Romney family. "What kind of a game is this anyway?"

"No game, Cord." Whit smiled slightly. "Sherry joined up at the last minute."

"He never signed on with me," protested Macklin. "He was wanted by the law back there, too."

"Didn't have time to sign with you, Cord," Whit said easily. "As for the law, you saw how that operates in Bedloe Landing. Dad'll stand in for Sherrill. I guess that's good enough." There was a murmur of assent from the spectators that caused Macklin's scowl to grow still blacker, but he said nothing further.

Whit stepped from the saddle and went to kneel at Sherrill's side. He said: "Give me a hand, boys."

Ed Deal, old Wilson, young Potter, and several others moved forward under Macklin's black glare. Together they picked Sherrill up and hoisted him into Whit's saddle, fitting his feet into the stirrups, supporting him as he sagged forward over the pommel. Regaining his senses a little, Sherrill gripped the saddle horn and held himself partially upright. Whit Romney took the rein and led the horse slowly away, the other men walking on either side to see that Sherrill did not fall.

Cord Macklin cracked his quirt viciously and bellowed like a bull: "All right, get the wagons movin'! We've wasted enough time on that deadwood. Gen 'em rollin' now!" His voice dropped off to a sullen mutter. "I'll break him like a rotten stick before the week is out. He won't last beyond Independence."

It was cool and dark when Sherrill came to again, and they were camped for the night, the wagons drawn into a great circle on the level plain, with campfires making red blurs about the enclosure and voices murmuring through the evening stillness. This time Sherrill seemed to be pillowed in comfort and security, and his mind was clearer although the pain pulsed and lingered in his head.

That blow must have been a severe one; when he tried to sit up he felt faint and dizzy. It wasn't necessary to hit a man that hard. Perhaps the one who had slugged him was an admirer of Nina Montez, and had poured some of his resentment against Sherry into the stroke. Lying back, Sherrill was able to smile at this notion. Overhead the stars looked large and close in the blue night sky, hanging in low brilliant clusters and swarms, and the moon was rising red-gold above distant mountain ramparts. The air was pure and good to breathe since the sun had gone and the dust settled.

His weakness filled him with a sense of failure, unpleasant in the extreme, and he concluded that part of it, at least, must have been caused by the dissolute life he had been leading. Perhaps this journey would be the best thing for him, after all. He hadn't spent much time in the saddle of late, and he understood now that he had missed it. Well, once his head cleared up it wouldn't take long to get toughened to the trail.

He was actually looking forward to long, hard days in the sun and wind, he discovered. It would be wonderful to feel fit and keen and strong once more. Then, recalling the pressure of Cord Macklin's powerful hands on him, Sherrill knew why it was that he wanted to condition himself to the strength, resilience and pliability to rawhide. The anger started his head to throbbing harder. He would have to kill Macklin, not only for Patch but for himself. He had felt it the first time he had seen the man.

Someone moved close beside him and a cool hand soothed his feverish brow. It was Molly Romney, her face clear and delicate in the starlight, her touch a comfort and a blessing. She brought him water, cold and fresh, the most delicious drink he had ever tasted. After drinking, he let her ease him back on the blankets and place a damp cooling cloth on his forehead. Without thought or effort Sherrill's hand sought the girl's and clung to it, and a strange sweet contentment came over him.

"I'm glad you're here," she said simply. "I'm sorry you were hurt, but I'm glad you are here."

"I reckon I am, too," he told her uncertainly. "I didn't think I wanted to come, but—Well, now it's different. Now I…" His voice trailed off, and Molly said he should rest and not try to talk. There was so much he wanted to say all of a sudden, but the words wouldn't come with any order or coherence. So he merely pressed her fingers, and her slight answering squeeze was enough for him—for a time. Then something intruded to break the spell.

It's just because I'm sick and weak, he thought. *It must be.... I'm not really glad to be here, not even with Molly and her family. This is no place for me to be. I belong in joints like the Royal and the River Belle, with all the whiskey and smoke and music and laughter, the lights and noise and women with painted faces, the rustle of pasteboards and click of dice, the quick flare-up of a fight with fists flying, guns flashing, bottles breaking, tables overturning. That is my world. And what in Tophet am I doing out here in the wilderness with these patient, plodding, honest pioneers? I'll go crazy! I'm no blasted pack animal. I'll never be able to stand the everlasting sameness and dullness, each day like the one before and the one coming.... Connover's to blame for this and some day I'll make him pay for it. Not with money but with blood, if there's any blood in that plump, smug little carcass of his.*

Sherrill had withdrawn his hand from Molly's. It was knotted into a fist now, and he was sweating in the blankets with that hammer pounding relentlessly in his skull.

"Whats is it, Sherry?" the girl asked anxiously. "What's the matter?"

"Nothing," he said tightly. "Nothing. I'm all right."

"Don't try to think or talk. Just relax, Sherry; rest easy. Mother is bringing you some broth."

"I can't eat."

"You'll like this, Sherry."

Later, after he had forced down as much of the excellent broth as possible, the other Romneys gathered around for a brief reassuring interval and Sherrill began to feel somewhat better. Their quiet, pleasant manner and their sincere friendliness gave him a renewal of spirit and faith. Some of their gentle calmness seemed to flow into his own bloodstream and quell the turbulence there. His thoughts lost their bitter edge and violence, started coursing smooth and placid and deep. He settled back in the new-found peace that the Romneys somehow had transferred to him, and Molly's hand found his once again as the others moved away.

It was like coming home at last after years of aimless wandering and wanton wildness. He fell asleep finally with the girl's hand still clasped in his.

CHAPTER EIGHT

It required two more days for Sherrill's head to clear, and he began to fret and chafe at the enforced idleness. But rest was what he needed, along with the fine food provided by Mrs. Romney and a total abstinence from liquor. It startled him a little to realize that this was the first period in years in which he had gone for days without whiskey.

At odd moments he craved a drink, but he put down the desire and mentioned it to no one. At times he was lonesome for the old devil-may-care life and the gay companions of saloons and gambling houses, for sauve Harry Connover and vivid Nina Montez, even for the tempestuous and treacherous Lilli Lavery. But as the miles rolled away the luster of those things dimmed and faded, and if he thought of anybody back in Bedloe it was the stricken Patch.

The trail followed the winding Missouri River as far as Independence, and it was smooth and easygoing. When he was up and around Sherrill started making friends with the splendid sorrel stallion Connover had supplied for him. "Big Red," he called him, and it was exhilarating to swing into the saddle and feel all that superb power under him.

Sherrill also felt better when he had buckled on his gun belt once more, and placed that beautiful Henry rifle in the saddle boot. He was ready then for Cord Macklin and Spicer and Koogle, but they were keeping strictly away from him. The Romneys were highly respected, and that probably saved Sherrill from immediate conflict with Macklin and his lieutenants.

Sherrill had been right in picking out the other two that night in front of the River Belle. Spicer was sharp and narrow as a hatchet, with a thin, pock-marked face, something evil about the gashed mouth and slit eyes, a weasel of a man. Koogle was large and floridly handsome, with crisp-curling brown hair, alert and quick in spite of his size, smiling and affable on the surface with the false cheer of a salesman, vindictive and ruthless underneath, very self-assured and superior. These two were seldom far away from the big boss Macklin.

Sherrill was pleasantly surprised to learn that, in a last-minute switch, Filchock had been replaced by a one-eyed veteran scout named McLowry, whom Sherry knew by reputation as an honest, reliable plainsman and a skilled and fearless Indian fighter. The sodden Filchock would have been easily dominated by Macklin, but not so the tough little McLowry. Sherrill was unwilling to believe that McLowry could have sold out to Lavery, but of Macklin and his associates he stood ready to expect anything.

The wagon train went on through days of sun and sand and scourging winds. Sherrill was riding and working with the Romney men now, gaining daily in strength and weight, taking satisfaction in the new tone and fiber of his muscles and the fresh clarity of his head. Burned by the sun and whipped by the wind into lean, leathery fitness, Sherry discovered an elation far better than the short-lived brand derived from drink. This was genuine, solid, down-to-earth. It had the qualities of the Romney family, and you did not have to pay the next morning for the half forgotten merriment of the night before.

It was a strange new world to Sherrill, however, and he was not able to adapt himself at once. In spite of the Romneys, there were spells of black depression and morbid loneliness, times when he would have given almost anything to be back in town pushing the swing-doors into the Royal or the River Belle or the Waterfront. To hear the men hailing him on all sides, to see the eyes of the women light up as they looked at him.

Maybe the glitter was tinsel and cheap, but he still missed it, now and then. You can't shake off the habits and customs of a hell-for-leather lifetime overnight; you have to grow away from them gradually. Sherrill was doing this, and he was not without gratitude for the opportunity, but he had his bad moments on the trail. Molly always knew, when his smile became absent and his amber eyes remote. Then she would touch his arm or shoulder and turn away, realizing that it was something he had to face and fight out by himself, alone.

The people of the train did not accept Sherrill too readily, even though he was a friend of the Romneys, almost like one of the family. For one thing, he was despised by Cord Macklin, and most of the emigrants regarded Macklin's judgment as infallible and irrevocable. For another, there was Sherrill's gaudy record as a gunman, gambler, and lover of loose women, an outlawed killer with a price on his head. Such ill fame naturally did not endear him to the sober, respectable, law-abiding family folks of the wagons.

They watched him narrowly and waited for some wild outbreak, some lawless demonstration on Sherrill's part, and the faithful wives and envious daughters declared that no good would come of Molly Romney's keeping company with that young Sherrill. It was a shame and a disgrace and something ought to be done about it. But nothing was.... And Sherrill went on acting as nice and quiet and gentlemanly as the Romney brothers themselves.

As the long, weary miles smoked and creaked away under the plodding hoofs and groaning axles, there developed a change in the way people spoke of Sherrill. "I don't put much stock in all them stories about him," they told one another. "He ain't nowhere near as bad as they paint him. Why, you couldn't ask for a nicer, pleasanter young fellah than Sherrill. Anyway, I figger if he's good enough for the Romneys he's good enough for me or anybody else."

And they said: "He's good with horses and cattle, and just you pay attention to how all the kids and dogs like him and follow him around. You can't fool kids and dogs nohow. Sherry minds his own business, but he's always ready to help with a broken wheel or tongue, to fetch water and round up stray cattle, to ride outpost more'n his share and stand sentry at night.

"They can say what they want to," they said, "but that Sherry's a good boy. He was maybe a little wild once, but all real boys have a streak of that in 'em. I ain't condemnin' that boy on hearsay, and I don't want nobody else runnin' him down neither. If it comes to a fight out here, we'll likely thank the good Lord we got Sherry on our side!"

By the time they were approaching Independence the majority of the emigrants had managed to make Sherrill understand that he was accepted at last, and welcome. Their rough little gestures of friendship pleased him more than he would have thought possible. Many subtle changes were taking place in Sherrill as he settled into the routine grind of the open road. Without being aware of it, he was slowly absorbing some of the simple strength, faith and courage of these homebuilders in the West.

He no longer resented Harry Connover's duplicity in shipping him out with the wagons. He began to look back upon his life in Bedloe Landing and points south with sharp distaste and shame. Sherrill knew regret now for all the wastrel years and the wasted time. In fulfillment of Harry Connover's prediction, he came to see this trip across the plains as the first worthwhile mission of his whole mad career.

Independence was the last outpost of civilization, and not very civilized at that, the jumping off place. Here the wagon trains stopped to buy additional provisions and make necessary repairs, and here the sick, injured, and fainthearted dropped out of the ranks. The Santa Fe Trail branched to the southwest; the Great Salt Lake Trail, which they were taking, diverged northwest toward the remote Rockies.

They made camp near the settlement where so many preceding caravans had bivouacked. Everyone wanted to get into Independence because it was the last town they would strike this side of the Rocky Mountains. Fort Kearney and Fort Laramie were military posts and nothing more.

Sherrill and the Romney brothers were among those who bathed in the Missouri River, shaved with care, and dressed in clean new range outfits for the evening. To avoid being conspicuous Sherrill wore only one gun. In strange towns there was always somebody ready to challenge any newcomer who packed two guns, and Sherrill didn't want any trouble tonight.

Independence, still partially surrounded by a crumbling stockade, had a wild raw frontier aspect as they walked in through the early darkness. The town was wide open whenever a wagon train arrived, the saloons, stores and eating places bright with garish lamplight and crowded with eager people. This was the last stop and emigrants always made the most of it, pouring their money across the bars, counters and gambling tables.

Sherrill and the Romney boys had a couple of beers on the outskirts and sauntered on toward the center of the community and the Ox-Bow Saloon, which seemed to be the principal rendezvous. They were perhaps twenty feet from the entrance when a red-headed giant swaggered out with four men at his heels, two nearly as large as himself, one very small with a double gun belt, and one a lanky string-bean sort of fellow.

The big redhead strode straight at them and thrust a solid shoulder into Sherrill with sufficient force to stagger him into a half-turn. "What the devil?" muttered Sherrill. The giant wheeled on him with ponderous might.

"When you see the Jessops comin' stand aside, brother!"

A sudden flame seared away all Sherrill's good intentions for the evening. It was as natural as breathing for his left hand to lash out into that heavy face. The giant's hat flew off and his red head rocked with the impact. The two big men crowded the Romney brothers against the saloon wall, mumbling something about fair play. String-bean and the small one stood off with thumbs hooked into gun belts, their faces frozen and expressionless.

"Ah, a fightin' rooster," said the red-headed man with gloating satisfaction. "Give us room, boys, and keep the crowd off." He spat blood and grinned, a dark flow staining his chin as he advanced on Sherrill.

Here we go again, thought Sherrill. *Why do they always pick on me?* He looked slender, youthful, almost frail before the rugged bulk of the red-headed Jessop, and he knew his chances would be thin if the giant got in close enough to grapple with him. A ring of spectators had formed instantly, and one of them said: "It's Big Jess! He'll kill that poor kid!"

Sherrill was swinging when Jessop charged, and a long-drawn gasp came from the onlookers at the lightning speed of his hands. Striking left and right, the reports ringing in swift stunning succession, Sherrill slashed the big man's face and drove him backward. The red head jerked from side to side under the smashing fists, and the ugly face was one glistening sheen of blood.

But Big Jess refused to go down, and as Sherrill came crouching in at him the giant finally unleashed and landed one terrible blow. Sherrill, feeling as if his head were torn from his shoulders, was flung crashing back into the wall of the Ox-Bow with such impetus that the breath was beaten from his body and consciousness nearly left his brain. Desperately he hung there, gasping for air, while the universe revolved about him in fiery sickening circles.

Laughing and blowing blood, Jessop moved in, apelike, to crush and mangle him against the side of the building, and everybody including the Romneys thought it was all over. But before those huge hands reached him Sherrill catapulted himself forward with flashing fists. Big Jess straightened up and tottered back as every shot Sherrill threw found its mark.

The red head bobbed and swayed as if unhinged and Jessop reeled across the boardwalk under those flogging hands. Sherrill set his feet and exploded one last whiplashing punch, lifting every ounce of his hundred and eighty pounds into it. Big Jessop's legs caught the hitch-rail and he went over backward, the red head thumping the dirt first, the massive shoulders settling into the dust, and his boots still across the rack.

A voice cut through the general confusion: "All right, Little Jess and Slim! They don't need no help from you!"

It was McLowry, the scout, a gun in each hand covering the small Jessop and the thin, lanky one. McLowry, with that black patch over his eyeless socket and his scarred leathery jaws munching a chew of tobacco. Little Mac, who knew Independence and the Jessops and had watched the whole thing, waiting for those two to go for their guns in case Big Jess couldn't do it with his bare hands.... And beside McLowry loomed fat Ed Deal, with his carbine lined on the two large men who had been blocking the Romneys to keep them out of action.

Big Jess was getting up slowly now, shaking his red head like a stunned ox, blood streaming down his ruined face and thick neck. Sherrill stood quietly waiting for him, thinking that he would be dead or dying now with bullets in his back, if it hadn't been for McLowry and Deal.

"Enough?" Sherrill inquired.

Jessop looked at him and snorted: "I ain't no glutton."

McLowry spoke again. "You Jessops oughta know better than to jump anybody from one o' my trains."

Big Jess peered at him from bruised, closing eyes. "Why, Mac, I didn't know you was on this one. Heard it was Filchock."

McLowry spat and smiled bleakly. "I don't know what's kept you boys alive this long. Dust off now before my trigger finger gets nervous." He glanced at Sherrill and the Romney brothers with a different kind of smile. "Let's drift back to camp, boys.

Ed and I laid in a stock o' whiskey and beer. We can drink more peaceful out there."

"That's right, boys," laughed Ed Deal. "This fightin' wastes a whole lot o' drinkin' time."

"You all right, Sherry?" asked Whit Romney.

Sherrill nodded. "Except for my neck being about a foot longer." He was bleeding a bit from mouth and nose and his head still rang, but his battered, aching hands hurt worse than anything else.

"We were a lot of help!" Whit said bitterly. "We might as well have been home in bed."

Jud said nothing, but his dark face was sullen with self-reproach.

McLowry said: "You boys thought it was just a stand-up fight. Don't be blamin' yourselves for anythin'."

They walked out toward the camp on the banks of the Missouri, the moonlight turning the earth to silver under their boots.

"What was that all about in there, Mac?" Sherrill asked.

McLowry chortled softly. "It's an old story in Independence, that Jessop bunch. Big Jess, Little Jess, Slim Jess, and them other jaspers, they're in business, you might say. If there's somebody on a wagon train you wanta get rid of, you see the Jessops and point the party out, and you pay their price. Then Big Jess picks a fight with this party, and most generally that's the end of it. When Big Jess gets done with 'em they ain't goin' across the prairies or nowhere else exceptin' a hospital or a graveyard. If the gent turns out too tough—like Sherrill here—Little Jess and Slim cut him down with their guns. But that don't happen much; Big Jess is usually enough.

"They been gettin' away with this for years, but they don't bother any train o' mine if they know I'm scoutin' it. A while back they beat a coupla boys 'most to death, and we drug 'em out to camp to learn 'em a lesson. Lashed 'em out to wagon wheels and whipped 'em senseless. They'll carry them marks the rest o' their days—may they be short ones. But it didn't seem to improve their character any. Somebody oughta kill 'em, but nobody ever gets around to doin' it."

"Then somebody must have paid them to tackle me?" mused Sherrill.

"I reckon so," McLowry drawled.

In camp they settled down to talk and drink in comfort around Ed Deal's fire. Sherrill stuck to the beer and left the whiskey for the others. McLowry's one eye lighted with pleasure as he tipped the bottle up. Men said that Mac's one eye had supernatural telescopic vision. The other eyeball had been gouged out in some frontier fight, it was said, which had ended with McLowry's opponent not only eyeless but earless. McLowry knew the plains, the mountains, and the Indians, and he had guided many wagon trains safely over the long train west. Sherrill was glad of this chance to get acquainted with the hard-bitten little scout.

"So far this trip's been too danged quiet and peaceable," said McLowry. "It ain't natural and it ain't to my likin'. Somethin's bound to break, and it'll sure be bad when it does."

"You had any trouble with Macklin?" asked Sherrill.

The one eye scrutinized him shrewdly. "No, not yet. But I'm liable to 'most any time. Up to now he's given me my head, but he don't like it none."

Sherrill laughed. "He's going to be disappointed to find me still around."

"I reckon," McLowry said. "He'll be tryin' somethin' else, Sherry."

"There's somethin' gone sour in Macklin," said Ed Deal. "I ain't got the same feelin' for him I used to have. I ain't had it since Cord quirted that boy blind in Natchez."

"That was a friend of mine," Sherrill said. "Macklin doesn't know it, though. I don't want him to until I'm ready to tell him."

They were all staring at Sherrill's lean face in the firelight. McLowry said: "I met a friend o' yours once down the river. A boy called Patch. Him and me and a soldier named Ehlers had ourselves quite a spree down in New Orleans."

"Patchin," said Sherrill. "He's the one."

McLowry went rigid. "Great Gawdamighty!" he said softly. "And his wife, Veronica?"

"She's dead, Mac."

McLowry was silent, with bent head, gazing into the slow flames. Finally he said: "Macklin have a hand in that, too?"

"That's right."

The one eye flashed up and the scarred cheeks twisted. "I knew that Macklin had to die the minute I sighted him, son."

"So did I," said Sherrill. "And he will—when we hit Fort Bridger."

"If not before," McLowry said. His single eye scanned the circle. "None o' this goes any further, boys."

Ed Deal snorted. "Not very likely, Mac!" The Romney brothers simply nodded in agreement.

McLowry slapped his buckskin-clad leg and reached for a bottle. "Get out that mouth-organ o' yours, Ed, and let's have some music."

CHAPTER NINE

ndependence and the Missouri were behind them now, civilization was behind them, as they drove cross-country in a northwesterly direction toward Fort Kearney on the Platte River. They reached Kearney, a pitifully undermanned little garrison in the wilderness, in due time and without any extraordinary incidents. From there the trail followed the Platte to Fort Laramie, a long, hard trek.

A week out of Kearney McLowry invited Sherrill to accompany him on a scouting foray. They were in Indian country now, Apache and Cheyenne territory. Sherry promptly threw the saddle on Big Red and joined the guide. As they rode past Cord Macklin's lead wagon they could feel the eyes of Spicer and Koogle boring into their backs, but Cord himself was not in evidence. They cantered on in silence and were miles ahead of the train before McLowry broke it.

"Well, son, that trouble we mentioned has come."

"What is it, Mac?"

"Macklin wants to leave the Platte and by-pass Laramie. There's a fork up ahead. It is shorter to the south, but right dangerous. A tough climb, and even worse goin' down the other side. This time o' year the waterholes are apt to dry up. I told Macklin, but he's dead set on the South Branch instead o' the North Bend to Laramie."

"It's crazy to leave the trail and the river," Sherrill said.

"Sure, it's crazy," muttered McLowry. "I'm beginnin' to think Cord Macklin is too."

"Couldn't we put it to a vote?"

"Wouldn't do any good. Cord'd swing it his way if it came to votin'. Them people still look up to Macklin. Even the Romney boys' folks'd likely vote his way."

Sherrill had told nobody, not even Whit Romney, but he decided to give it point-blank to the little scout. "Mac, you knew Jay Lavery of the River Belle. Did you know he was betting this train wouldn't go through to Bridger?"

McLowry nodded simply and grinned at Sherrill's astounded look. "Yes, I know, son. I reckon that's why I'm here."

"What do you mean, Mac?"

"Well, Harry Connover never had too much regard for Filchock as a scout. That last night in Bedloe somebody lured Fiddle into the Royal and kept loadin' uncommonly powerful drinks into him. The Fiddler never could resist free liquor, and he swilled enough to paralyze himself for at least a week. I reckon maybe Harry told his bartenders to keep Fiddle's glass filled up as long as Fiddle could hold it. When the Fiddler passed out Harry tipped me to this job and mentioned a bonus, seein' as how he was bettin' against Lavery. My money was about gone and I was about ready to take another train out, so I took it."

Sherrill laughed until he was rocking in the saddle, and McLowry chortled along with him. "That Connover!" said Sherrill. "That slick, smooth son-of-a-gun, he never misses a trick. He passed Filchock out to keep him off the train, and he knocked me out to put me on it!"

"A good swap—for our side," grinned McLowry. "He's a smart one, that Harry. And honest, too, for a gamblin' man."

They reached the place where the trail diverged, and looked around. There were no fresh signs on the ground. The main route swung northward along the Platte River, safe and an assured water supply beyond Laramie. Mc Lowry's one eye was bitter as he gazed at the wild, broken country and the rocky height of land to the southwest.

"I don't like it," McLowry grumbled. "That South Branch is a bad one, always has been. Nobody takes it any more since that Selway bunch was wiped out on the Ottaquechee."

"We'll make a stand against Macklin when we get back," said Sherrill. "We can't leave the river, Mac."

"Won't do much good prob'ly," muttered McLowry. "But we'll try it. Maybe give Macklin and Koogle and Spicer somethin' to think about."

They had turned their horses back to the east when suddenly the air hummed and whined with lead as bullets beat up the dust around them and rifles cracked in the distance. Veering wider apart and hanging low in the saddle, McLowry and Sherrill threw their horses into a hard gallop. There was another scattering of shots and then silence save for the pounding hoofs. Peering back, the riders saw only faint smoke puffs thinning along a rocky escarpment in the northwest. Safely out of range, they slowed to a walk, the horses already lathered and blowing in the heat.

"Long shootin'," said McLowry. "And pretty good for Indians—too good."

"Have they got rifles that powerful?" asked Sherrill.

"They've got 'em, some of 'em. But they don't come that close with 'em."

"Then? ..." Sherrill felt his dry lips thin tautly on his teeth.

"It wasn't Indians," finished McLowry. "I been expectin' somethin' like this."

"We could find out who's away from the wagons."

McLowry shook his head. "No good. The usual pointers and flankers are out."

"Maybe they're just playing." Sherrill grinned without humor.

"Maybe," McLowry said, and spat viciously into the buffalo grass.

They watered their horses in the Platte, drank thirstily themselves, and loped back along the broad, sun-baked valley. They met the train with Cord Macklin riding along at the head, bulking big and dark in the saddle with that thick quirt looped on his wrist. They turned to ride alongside of him.

"Well?" he demanded impatiently. "See anythin'?"

"No," said McLowry. "But we was fired on at the fork."

"What do you expect?" Macklin said. "We're gettin' deep into Indian territory. Where'd the shots come from, north or south?"

"West," answered McLowry. "And north."

"All the more reason for takin' the South Branch."

"There's no reason for takin' that route," McLowry insisted. "If it was Indians, they'd play it that way to drive us south into ambush."

"Talk sense, man!" barked Cord Macklin. "Who'd it be if it wasn't Indians?"

"That," drawled McLowry, "I don't know. I still say the North Bend and stick to the river."

"And we still go south," Macklin said, twisting abruptly in his saddle to face Sherrill. "What have *you* got to say, mister?"

"North," said Sherrill with a dim smile.

Cord Macklin laughed and eyed the quirt in his great hand. "Some day, mister, I'll change that pretty smile for you! All right, you can get along now." He dismissed them with a contemptuous flick of the whip, and they drifted on down the long laboring line of dust-drenched wagons.

"I want to be there the day you take *him,* Sherry," Mc Lowry said, an almost prayerful note in his voice.

When they came to the Romney Conestoga, they found anxious looks drawn on the faces of the entire family, and fear in the eyes of the parents and Molly. Sickness had struck the wagon next in line, owned by the Wilsons, some strange malady that defied diagnosis and brought the dread of an epidemic.

The mother and three younger children were bedded down in the wagon, utterly helpless and sobbing painfully for air, their faces inflamed and bloated. The father and the two bigger boys were carrying on as best they could, sick themselves but working on nerve and will-power, with the Romneys, Potters and other nearby families offering all the assistance possible.

"They'll never make the South Branch," murmured Mc Lowry. "It's rough and steep and hard goin', up and down both. And there isn't even a fort between here and Bridger."

"It gives us something to work on with the others," Sherrill said grimly. "If I can convince the Romneys we'll be able to swing some weight against Macklin."

Sharply and concisely Sherrill laid the facts before the Romney family, talking faster, more forcefully and earnestly than ever before, straining and driving to make them see the situation as he saw it, without accusing Macklin outright of plotting betrayal. Impetuous Whit sided at once with Sherrill. The more conservative Jud weighed the question with scrupulous care before joining them. Mr. Romney, still somewhat dubious and averse to crossing Cord Macklin, was finally swayed by the piteous moans and wails from the Wilson wagon and the urging of his wife and daughter.

"Yes, I think Cord is wrong to leave the Platte and the main trail," Mr. Romney admitted at last. "I can't understand his making such a choice. It's against all reason and common sense."

"Now we've all got to spread the word," Sherrill said. "And we've got to work fast."

They did, scattering up and down the column, appealing to one family after another. Sherrill, McLowry and the three Romneys talked to the men, while Molly sought support among the women.

"It's *your* wagon train!" Sherrill told them. "It belongs to you and your families, not to Macklin. It'll be murder to drag the Wilsons away from the river over the South Branch, and there'll be others dying if we leave the Platte and go Macklin's way. Bring your guns to the lead wagon and stand together for the North Bend for Fort Laramie."

All along the line were men of pride and spirit, who had long since begun to fret inwardly at the high-handed, slave-driving tactics of Cord Macklin, Spicer and Koogle. They caught fire from Sherrill and the Romneys, and rallied strongly to the cause. And even those who were deathly afraid of Macklin were still more afraid of leaving the Platte River and the main route.

As the lead wagon neared the fork a mounted delegation drew up alongside of it, followed by scores of other armed men on foot. Cord Macklin swung down to face them as the train ground to a stop in the billowing dust, and Koogle and Spicer took their places on either side of the trail boss.

"What is this?" roared Cord Macklin, his hawk face blackening with anger. "Get back to your wagons, you men!"

It was Mr. Romney who dismounted and replied to him, much to Macklin's surprise and consternation. "We've called a halt, Cord. We want to talk this over before we go on." The Romney brothers, Sherrill, McLowry, Ed Deal, and other riders stepped down and ranged themselves behind their spokesman. Young Potter was there, supporting old Wilson, who was barely able to stand.

"There's nothin' to talk about!" shouted Macklin, the cords standing out in his neck. "I'm bossin' this outfit. Get the blazes back where you belong!" But he was obviously taken aback to find Mr. Romney heading the opposition.

"We still have the right to speak our minds, Cord," Mr. Romney reminded him in his mild, grave tones. "We're still free men."

Cord Macklin slashed the air with his whip. "All right; speak up then. What do you want here?"

"We want to stay on the river and the main trail to Laramie. The majority wants it, Cord. You can call a vote if you like."

"The devil with a vote! Don't you know it's a hundred miles longer that way? Maybe more'n a hundred."

"It's also safer, easier, and the water supply is constant," said Mr. Romney. "There's a sick family in the line, Cord. They might make it to Fort Laramie, but they aren't ready for that South Branch."

"What family is sick, the Wilsons?" demanded Macklin. "The Wilsons! They're nothin' but weaklin's anyway; they never shoulda started this trip. Why didn't they drop out at Independence or Kearney?" His voice rose to a mighty bellow. "You know the, law of the trail! One wagon never holds up the whole train!"

"We prefer the law of humanity," Mr. Romney said gently. "We can all go together on the regular Salt Lake Trail. There's no need to leave a sick family to die in this wilderness."

In sudden towering rage Cord Macklin turned on Sherrill. "This is all your doin', mister! I shoulda cut you down the first time I ever saw you!" The cruel quirt was dancing on his brawny wrist.

"Start cutting now," invited Sherrill, standing tall and loose and easy, big hands hanging near the gun butts on his thighs, thinking as he waited: *Perhaps this is it. I hope so; it's been too long a wait already. Perhaps this is it, Patch boy....*

Macklin's bulking frame tensed and quivered, and for a breathless space held that tension, until it was nearly unbearable to every man rooted there in the desert dust and glare. Then he relaxed and drew back a step, and just as men started to breathe once more Macklin placed two fingers in his mouth and whistled a piercing blast.

Immediately two bearded men with guns in either hand sprang from the lead wagon. It was fantastic, so unreal, so incredible, so much like a stage play, that the amazed audience could only stand and stare in stupefaction as the bearded gunmen lined up beside Macklin.

Sherrill recognized them instantly. Even the thick growth of whiskers failed to disguise the long, mournful mountain-preacher features of Mitchum, and the bullneck and tough, brutal face of tobacco-chewing Holway. So this was Lilli Lavery's trump card, two ace killers in the hole, insurance on her wager and reassurance that the wagon train would be wrecked and lost before Fort Bridger. He wondered when and where they had overtaken the train. Probably at Independence or Kearney. Most likely they had trailed it at a respectful distance until Macklin had called them in to be on hand for this showdown at the fork.

Spicer and Koogle now had their weapons unlimbered, and Cord Macklin was smiling darkly in triumph. Holway, who had always wanted to get Sherrill, could scarcely control his trigger fingers now that Sherry was under his guns.

"Gimme the word," panted Holway, eyes hungry on Sherrill. "Lemme turn 'em loose on Pretty Boy, Cord!"

"Shut up, Holway!" Cord Macklin said curtly. "Do any of you men still wanta argue the point?" He laughed, but Sherrill detected a certain strain in it. Cord leaned toward Mr. Romney and said, low-voiced: "Sorry to have to use such methods, but it's best for all of us. We got to have order and discipline." Then Cord Macklin broke into a thunderous roar: "All right, men, back to your wagons! Back to your jobs. Get 'em rollin' again. We're takin' the South Branch!"

The long line of wagons lurched away from the peaceful Platte River and creaked over a little traveled trail, rough and tortuous, toward that ominous barrier rearing against the southwest skyline.

Three days later Mrs. Wilson and her three small children died in the blinding noontide heat, while the men and beasts were sweating and straining, pushing and hauling and heaving their hearts out to get the wagons over the steep, rocky heights.

That night one of the older Wilson boys was crushed under an overturned Pittsburgh as they slipped and slithered, plunged, skidded and careened crazily down the other side of the mountain. It was morning when they got the lad's pulped body out of the wreckage. Old Man Wilson took one look at it, grabbed his ancient Springfield, and went snarling and stumbling on fever-ridden legs after the lead wagon. But Holway saw him blundering down the pass with the rifle. Drawing calmly, Holway shot him calmly through the heart before he could get to Cord Macklin.

The other boy, the last of the Wilsons, blew his own head off when the wagons reached the waterhole at the bottom and found it bone-dry and covered with sand and silt.

CHAPTER TEN

As the days passed the water supply ran low. All the water-holes along the South Branch had dried up, and the streams that McLowry remembered were nothing but dry beds of stone rapidly filling with dirt. There was nothing to do but ration the scant water and push on toward the Rocky Mountains, that never seemed to get any nearer.

The heat increased as the train snaked slowly across the arid expanses of wasteland, and blistering winds and flying sand added to the torture of the travelers. There was more sickness as people gave themselves over to despair, and morale ebbed lower from day to day. An aged woman and two more children died and were buried on the scorched plains, with time for little if any ceremony. People began to tell one another that the dead were fortunate, that the dead were better off than the living.

By now Cord Macklin's stock had dropped to rock bottom, and he was never seen alone. Holway and Mitchum alternated as bodyguards with Koogle and Spicer. Rumor had it there was still plenty of water cached in the lead wagon, and indeed the five men there seemed less in need than the rest, but nobody knew for certain. And there was no means of finding out unless they raided the Macklin wagon. A free-for-all battle at this time would destroy what small chance the wagon train had of survival, as Sherrill pointed out repeatedly to men who were maddened by the agony of their womenfolk and children.

There were occasional suicides along the line as the hideous nightmare went on until minds were deranged and unbalanced.

Young Potter, crazed by the suffering thirst of his wife and baby, went berserk and started for the lead wagon one sweltering afternoon. Men tried to stop him, but Potter burst free with insane strength and went reeling on, gripping his Winchester.

Cord Macklin saw him coming, a scarecrow figure stumbling in his weakness and mad haste, brandishing the rifle. Koogle smiled and trained his revolver on the wretched creature, but Cord Macklin struck it down and waited calmly, hoping Potter would fire at least one wild shot before Spicer got him.

Potter staggered closer, screaming and raising the rifle: "Die now, you black murderin' monster! Die, blast your soul, die!"

The rifle barrel was wobbling level when Spicer, the weasel, stepped out from between two wagons behind Potter and shot him twice through the back. And it was young Potter who died, his cracked swollen mouth working against the desert floor until a final crimson gush stilled it.

Learning of this, friends of the Potters were for lifting their guns in outright revolution, and Sherrill felt like it himself but knew it would be folly. With the help of Mc Lowry and the Romneys, he managed to restrain and quiet them before Cord Macklin and his men came stalking down the row.

"Not yet, not now," Sherrill said. "The time will come."

Drawing abreast of the stricken group, Cord Macklin announced: "Too bad, folks, but it couldn't be helped. The man was out of his head, insane and dangerous. It had to be done, that's all."

Sunken eyes turned to watch Macklin and his trained killers swagger along the line, teeth showed in haggard, sunburned faces, and knuckles jutted whitely as grimy hands tightened on weapons. But Sherrill held them in check, because if it started now the slaughter would be great and indiscriminate, and the whole expedition might perish as a result. They needed all the man-power they had to keep the wagons moving.

"There's a chance I know of, a waterin' place in the hills," said McLowry, a faraway look in his one eye. "The train couldn't ever get to it, but a scoutin' party could. It's the only chance we got, Sherry."

They plodded on in blind agony through a blazing inferno that seemed boundless. More people died and found shallow graves in the sun-hardened soil, the old and unwell and the infants. Then horses and cattle started to expire, and there were innumerable halts while they were cut loose and left along the way, with the bones of other wagon trains bleached white in the sun. In most of the pioneers' minds every death was charged directly to Cord Macklin's account.

They made a last-hope camp at the point McLowry estimated was the nearest they could attain to his watering place in the hills. As the wagons deployed left and right to form the vast circle, men and animals floundered and fell to their knees in sheer exhaustion. There was no going on without water, that was only too obvious. With a supply from the hills they might make the next waterhole on the South Branch. Without it there was no chance whatsoever; they were lost and doomed and done for, with death merely a matter of anguished time.

There was a stern council of war that evening, with parched and aching throats precluding any unnecessary talking, and stark figures standing or squatting with rifles ready or hands on gun butts. In some way Sherrill had gradually assumed leadership here, and even Macklin and his men listened as Sherry urged that they forget all differences until they were out of this valley of death. Under the spell of his quiet, easy voice, listeners relaxed a little and loosed the grip on their guns. Harmony being established for the moment, McLowry described briefly his plan for securing water, and the group set about selecting members to comprise his detail.

It was eventually agreed that the party, to be led by McLowry in the morning, would consist of Spicer and Holway from the lead wagon, Sherrill and Whit Romney from the ranks, and two pack-horses for each rider with all the containers possible to carry.

Sherrill had said good night to Molly and was getting ready to crawl into his blankets, near the sleeping Romney brothers, when McLowry slipped in soundlessly out of the shadows and handed him a pair of folded papers.

"Just in case, Sherry," whispered the scout. "Maps for you and Whit. Maybe you can read 'em after I run over it with you."

They crouched beside the dying fire and McLowry quickly pointed out the significant features on one of his crude maps. Sherrill, trying to concentrate and catch every point, was vaguely disturbed by a sense of fondness and fear for the leather-tough little man at his side. A man who knew Patch and Steve Ehlers, and who had saved Sherry's life in Independence.

"Mac, why don't you sleep in here with us?" he asked.

"Heck, I sleep with one eye open!" McLowry grinned and spat into the embers, winking his single eye. "I ain't worried, Sherry. I'll be all right. Just figgered it's better to have three of us knowin' how to get to that water." He clapped Sherrill soundly on the back and moved away from the fireside into the darkness.

At daybreak Sherrill woke with a scream in his ears. Beside him the Romney brothers jerked upright. All three had buckled on their gun belts and grabbed their carbines before they were fully awake. On sleep-stiffened legs they ran toward the center of the commotion, sleepy eyes searching for danger signs in all directions. Everywhere men were climbing out of blankets or tumbling out of wagons and reaching for their rifles.

But apparently there was no cause for general alarm, although there was reason enough for grief and the loss to the expedition was inestimable. The guards had found a body outside the wagon ring, a woman had screamed on seeing them bring the corpse in. It was the scout, Mc Lowry, looking smaller than ever in death, his skull split by a tomahawk, the scalp-lock gone, and his one eye staring in blank accusation at the morning sky.

"Apaches!" rasped a man beside Sherrill. "They'll be comin' at us now, and we'll all end up like that!"

Sherrill put his hand on the man's shoulder. "Take it easy. You don't want to talk that way with women and kids around."

Fat Ed Deal blew through his whiskers. "I never saw Apaches ruin a scalp-lock that way before they took it."

"I know what you mean, Ed," said Sherrill. "But we'd better keep it quiet. For that matter, no Indian would ever get that close to Mac."

"You're darn right they wouldn't," Ed Deal said. "Never in a hundred years, Sherry."

Cord Macklin crowded into the clump of men around McLowry's body, eyes like black liquid fire, quirt snapping and flirting. Spicer, Koogle, Mitchum and Holway were close behind him.

"Well, there goes our water," Cord said. "Looks like the trail ends right here."

Sherrill looked at him. Cord's lips weren't parched and blackened, split and peeling, like everyone else's in the line. He was getting his water, and so were the other four in the front wagon. Sherrill said:

"We'll still get water. This may be the beginning of a new trail."

Cord Macklin eyed him with scorn. "You're goin' crazy like Potter did, mister? You think you're a scout now, huh? All right, then. Koogle will go along in place o' McLowry this mornin'. Break it up here, and some of you men get Mac underground."

Jud Romney stepped forward, quiet and dark and intense. "I'll go along too, Cord."

Macklin studied him and shrugged indifferently. "Go ahead if you wanta." He turned to Ed Deal. "You think it was Apaches?"

"Not unless they've changed. They never used to strike at night."

Macklin's black eyes pierced the fat man. Cracking the whip, he strolled casually back to his four gunmen.

Sherrill turned quickly and walked away. He couldn't look at Cord Macklin and those others any longer without risking throwing his guns on them.

Molly Romney had a cup of milk waiting for him. "Bad, Sherry?"

He nodded. "Yes, it gets worse all the time."

CHAPTER ELEVEN

Every able-bodied person in the encampment was out, watching with mingled hope and dread, when the six riders set forth that early forenoon. There were many who never expected to see any of the six again, but for the most part they were wise enough to conceal their fears.

Women wept and called on God to bless the riders. Men raised blackened fists to the rising sun and cheered hoarsely from dry throats. Children frolicked and shouted shrilly, with dogs romping and barking among them. The cattle were bawling for water, as they did now day and night, a mournful and unceasing sound. The wagons had a look of permanent desolation, as if they were settling into a final resting place in the seared and barren earth, forlorn and without hope of ever rolling onward.

It was a scene Sherrill would never forget, and sharpest of all he remembered the fine dark head and clear bronzed face of Molly Romney. The light in her tired gray eyes, the lift of the chin, the lovely line of her throat, and the brave smile that brought a stinging hurt across Sherrill's eyes as he waved farewell.

Mr. and Mrs. Romney stood side by side near their daughter, a prayer in their eyes as they lifted their hands; Mrs. Romney would hold back her tears until the riders were gone. The young Potter widow, baby in arms, sat on the wagon seat, and fat Ed Deal, her protector since Potter's death, leaned on the front wheel at her feet. Black Cord Macklin and dour Preacher Mitchum, Cord flicking the quirt fretfully, the Preacher slouched and brooding, stood well apart from the masses.

Now, miles north and deep in the sandy rocky scrub-covered hills, the six horsemen were not a unit but two hostile factions forced to travel together, wary and watchful of each other as well as of outside dangers. And distrust and hatred lay between them as they rode. Sherrill and the Romney brothers were on one side; Spicer, Koogle and Holway on the other. McLowry, who should have been leading the way, was dead and buried back there, and Sherrill was still shaken and embittered by the blow and the loss. There was no replacing little Mac.

Measuring the three from the lead wagon, Sherrill concluded that in a fair stand-up fight only Holway would be formidable, but Spicer was sly and poisonous, and Koogle was diabolical behind that smiling front. Those three were marked for death if ever men were. Koogle and Spicer had it coming on Patchin's behalf, and Spicer had added to his crimes with the cold-blooded murder of poor Potter. The tough Holway was a natural-born killer and a menace to society; his brutal slaying of old man Wilson was but one of many such misdeeds in Holway's bloody career as a hired gunman. And without question one of them had used the hatchet on McLowry last night. Yes, those three would have to die.

"They won't try anything until we locate the water," Sherrill told the Romney boys. "Natural enough, because they depend on us to find it. But after that we can expect trouble, and when it breaks, shoot to kill. You should have no more feeling about killing these men than you would have for three mad dogs." To impress this on them, Sherrill described in detail the fate of Veronica Patchin. Whit and Jud listened with teeth on edge, and surveyed their three foemen with a new and harsher interest.

It was difficult to pick out landmarks in this bleak, rolling wasteland, but McLowry had recorded them with photographic accuracy, and the keen eyes of Sherrill and Whit Romney traced the route from one to another. A rock pillar here, a boulder-strewn butte there, a triangular-shaped mesa ahead, a terrace of vari-colored stone layers in line with a distant northern peak. Under normal conditions, Mc Lowry had said, it was an average day's ride to their objective, but with men and horses alike suffering from thirst and badly travel-worn, they would have to press hard all the way to make it before dark. They were undernourished also, for with tongues and throats swollen from lack of water it was impossible to eat properly.

At regular intervals they paused to wet their tongues from canteens already half empty, and to swab the alkali dust from the nostrils and lips of the horses. As the afternoon wore on, with blast-furnace heat and the water sloshed lower in the canteens, it became a strictly personal matter for them to reach their goal. They had to have water in order to live. The wagon-train supply became secondary, if they thought of it at all. Their own burning, choking need was first, and nothing else mattered.

Sherrill was feeling it too, sinking back into his old selfish mode of thought, damning Harry Connover for casting him into such a predicament, damning even the Romneys and Patchin for having played any part in getting him involved in this hideous torture. Once he would never have had the patience and will and tenacious strength to endure it. He would have said, "The devil with this," and pulled his guns on those three, taking Holway first, then Spicer and Koogle; and they would all have died in a sudden explosion of flame and smoke, along with himself. But at least they would have been out of this horrible ordeal.

Now, however, Sherrill caught himself up, forced his thoughts back into line and controlled them firmly there. He was no longer a lone wolf, to live and fight and die as he chose. There were others, too many others, who figured in his life, who relied on his continuing existence for their own safety. Sherrill straightened in the saddle and stroked Big Red's wet, matted mane.

On they rode in the blazing heat, flayed raw and blistered, gagging on tongues grown too large for their mouths, sunblind and lightheaded and swaying in the saddle. Steadily and stubbornly they drove forward, the horses lathered and stumbling with wildly rolling eyes, on and on and on through that flaming inferno, each rider filled to the bursting point with his own misery and pain.

Whit and Jud Romney were taking it in stride, like the thoroughbreds they were: Whit grinned at Sherrill from time to time with burned, cracked lips, while Jud was patient and stolid. The lead wagon men, having enjoyed more water and food in the past week, were in better physical shape, but they were the first to show signs of breaking.

Koogle, who had formerly been big, fleshy and pompous, began to wilt and fold and complain as the lard streamed off him in the desert sun. "Turn back," he croaked. "For the love of heaven turn back! We'll all die out here, you fools!"

"They'll all die back there if we don't get them water," Sherrill said. "There's nothing to turn back for."

"There's some water," Koogle groaned. "A little water."

"In Macklin's wagon," said Sherrill. "But only enough for Macklin's boys."

Next it was Holway, the hard-case gunfighter, madness flaring in his eyes as he cursed everybody in the party and Sherrill in particular. As his brain fried and cooked, Holway could think of nothing but shooting Sherrill, until finally Sherry had to draw and keep Holway under his gun as they rode.

Spicer, the weasel, small and sharp and wiry, seemed surprisingly impervious to the elements and indifferent to the torment, alert and tireless and stoical. Spicer might be the dangerous one, at that, Sherrill realized. He seemed to have more stamina and will than his bigger, stronger companions.

The sun was low and red when Sherrill spotted the twin humps of a thinly wooded ridge that marked their destination. "There it is, boys," he said, pointing, well aware that they needed encouragement. In the northern distance the Snowy Range lifted frosty white pinnacles against the fading colors of the sky.

They were all reeling in the saddle, aching, groggy and beaten down with weariness, burned and crisped and shriveled, charred to a cinder dryness. Doggedly they urged the spent horses across the spare-grassed basin toward the ridge.

Holway thrust his bull-neck at Sherrill. "Now, if the water ain't there, Pretty Boy…"

"Hold your fool tongue, Holway," ordered Spicer.

Sherrill said, "It's there; I can almost smell it from here. Just like Mac said…. See the green over there?"

Their hearts went up a little as enmity was momentarily forgotten. The sun was gone before they gained the shelter of the twin humps. Evening flowed over them with blessed coolness, and it seemed very dark all at once. The soft rippling music of running water came to them, and nothing had ever sounded so sweet and good. Croaking inarticulate joy, they pushed onward through green-hazed shadow to the small stream.

"Not too much," warned Sherrill, restraining himself with the utmost effort while the others flung themselves down to drink and bathe their fiery encrusted faces.

Glancing aside, Sherrill saw that Spicer was also waiting and watching him, and their red-rimmed eyes met in a peculiar understanding look. Sherrill smiled stiffly, but Spicer's thin, pock-marked face did not alter. Yes, Spicer was his chief adversary now; the weasel was the one Sherrill must pit himself against.

When the others finished and moved slightly downstream to water the horses, Sherrill and Spicer took their turn. It was heavenly to bury one's face in that cold running water, but the temptation to drink too much was almost overpowering. When Sherrill ducked his sweaty head and, dripping, pulled away from the delicious current, Spicer was already upright, slitted eyes taking in the brush-covered, boulder-marked terrain.

"Don't let those horses overdrink, boys," called Sherrill.

Holway's sullen voice growled back: "Who in tarnation made you captain, Pretty Boy?"

They selected a camp site and prepared for the night. The horses were unsaddled and unpacked, sponged off and rubbed down, watered again and fed, tethered a safe distance from the creek. After stripping and bathing in pairs, the men dressed and ate sparingly of their rations. Lounging about the fire, they rolled cigarettes then, and for the first time in days could relish the taste of tobacco smoke. Bone-tired and burned out, they were all ready to turn in, but it was decided to keep a two-man guard throughout the night.

Koogle and Jud Romney were to take the first watch, Holway and Whit the second, Spicer and Sherrill the third and last. They would actually be on guard against one another more than against any outside forces, but it was nonetheless an essential procedure. Sherrill intended to stay awake all night if he could, figuring that Spicer would have the same idea for himself.

But Sherrill's heavy, dragging weariness outweighed his will. Sinking finally and irresistibly into sleep, his last thought was that it would be all right as long as Jud and Whit Romney were there....

In the night, it was as though some tremendous force snatched him bodily out of his sleep and left him stricken but awake, quivering all over and frozen with a nameless horror. When Sherrill could move, his hands went automatically to his guns, and he breathed only after finding the familiar grips.

The cold was not just inside him; it was outside, everywhere, penetrating the blankets with icy insistence. He caught the orange blur of the small fire before his eyes fully adjusted themselves, and then he saw the man slumped there, back against a boulder, and recognized the shapely blond head. Whit Romney, on the second watch, *but the boy was asleep!* Sherrill drew his guns, freed his arms from the blankets and wriggled to a half reclining posture on his elbows.

A shadow flitted toward the rear of the boulder on which Whit rested, and Sherrill thought with sudden panic: *Indians!*

The woods are probably full of them.... Then firelight struck red on the thin pocked face of Spicer, the weasel, and there was a hatchet in his upraised right hand, his slit eyes were fixed glitteringly on the bent golden head of Whit Romney, his mouth an evil downturned gash. *So Spicer was Macklin's hatchet-man, the murderer of Mc Lowry.*

Sherrill lifted his right-hand gun and fired. Spicer stopped and stiffened at the top of his stroke, the tomahawk dropping from his shattered right arm as he twisted around to seek his assailant. Sherrill was sitting up straight now with the gun steady across his bent knees. Spicer was reaching frantically with his left hand as Sherrill's .44 flamed again, and once more. The first slug smashed Spicer's breastbone, the second split that pock-marked face. The weasel sprawled back against a tree trunk, writhed about convulsively, and slid slowly to earth, broken arm and good one hugging the rough bark.

Whit Romney was on his feet now, whirling with carbine ready to watch Spicer embrace the foot of that tree in death. Jud was thrashing into wakefulness nearby when Sherrill kicked loose from his blankets and struggled to his knees. Koogle and Holway were nowhere in sight, and Sherrill shouted for Whit to get away from the fire.

As Sherrill reared upright, somebody crashed in through the underbrush in a wild charge at him. As he tried to dodge for cover, Sherrill's boots caught, tripping and throwing him violently as a gun blazed in his direction. It was Holway in a mad-bull rush, bent on realizing at last his ambition to kill Sherrill, failing because Sherry's feet became entangled in his own blankets.

Holway was almost on top of Sherrill, but before he could throw down on the man beneath him, Whit Romney had pumped three bullets into him from the Remington carbine, slamming Holway into a long sidewise stagger. Snarling like a wounded beast, Holway toppled over a log and pitched into the brush, rolling, kicking and wrestling with death, furious to the very finish.

Sherrill and Jud were up together now, with Whit beside them, and all three were crouching and searching for Koogle.

"Where are you, Koogle?" yelled Sherrill. "Your friends are dead here. You'd better come in with your hands up."

After an interval of silence Koogle's voice came quavering back from the outer darkness. "You won't kill me, will you? I had nothing to do with this, I swear. Don't shoot, boys, I'm coming in .... I'm coming in empty-handed."

Koogle came through the bushes like a bull moose and blundered out into the reddish glow of the campfire, hands outstretched with spread fingers, once handsome face carved in with terror, mouth agape, eyes bulging and hypnotized by fear.

"I don't like this," Sherrill muttered. "Why couldn't he come in shooting?"

Sheathing his guns and motioning the Romneys to stand off, Sherrill strode forward to confront the shivering hulk of a man. "Get your hands up," he said, stepping in close to unbuckle Koogle's gun belt, sick at the thought of dealing with such a craven.

Sherrill felt the sudden surge and heave of the bulk in front of him, even before he sensed the savage downswing of the right arm and heard the warning cries from Whit and Jud. Ducking low and dodging to his right, Sherrill drove his left fist wrist-deep into Koogle's soft-paunched belly and heard the gasping groan as the big man doubled forward. The knife, concealed somehow in Koogle's sleeve, had swished close enough to slice a shallow cut down Sherry's left shoulder.

Straightening swiftly and striding forward, Sherrill whipped his right to that sagging jaw, getting everything from his ankles up into the terrific blow. Koogle's big curly head snapped back on the plump neck, and he landed flat on his shoulder blades fifteen feet away, the knife flying out of his hand, a red-gleaming arc in the firelight.

Still conscious, Koogle heaved himself up into a sitting position, wagging his curly head and holding his broken jaw, spitting out mouthfuls of blood and splintered teeth. Sherrill picked Koogle's gun belt off the ground and tossed it at him. Koogle shook his head, scarlet pouring down his chin to stain the costly checkered shirt.

"I'm glad you had that knife," Sherrill told him. "Now you better reach for the gun, Koogle, because I'm going to kill you anyway. I promised a friend of mine named Patchin I would. You remember Patch—and Veronica?"

"No, no!" protested Koogle. "Cord and Spicer, not me. I never touched that woman!" Seeming to beg and grovel for mercy, Koogle suddenly reached with surprising quickness for the gun on the turf.

Sherrill scarcely appeared to move as he drew and his right side burst instantly into roaring flame. The first bullet broke Koogle's outflung arm and the next tore through his shoulder. Then Sherrill's left hand flashed and he opened up with the other Colt, hammering his shots straight across that broad abdomen, blasting the great hulk apart against the smoking firelit earth. The silence was strange and frightening after all the racket, and the stench of cordite hung heavy in the night.

"Well, I reckon that does it," Sherrill said wearily. "We're all right now, boys. If it doesn't bring the Apaches down on us."

"I went to sleep, Sherry," Whit Romney said bitterly. "I darned near got us all killed here."

"No sense worrying about that now, Whit," said Sherrill, reloading his guns. "It could have happened to anybody after a day like yesterday. It turned out all right, boy, so forget it. You shot Holway right off my back, you know. ... I suppose we'd better get rid of these bodies."

At sunset on the following day the three survivors rode into camp with a life-saving cargo of fresh water and three empty saddles. The terrible ordeal of the past thirty-six hours was written plainly in their sun-blackened, hollow-cheeked, sunken-eyed faces. They had aged years in the last day and a half.

As rapidly as possible water was distributed among the long-thirsting pioneers, with admonitions to be exceedingly frugal in its use. Spirits soared once more in the enclosure, and Sherrill and the Romney brothers were hailed as heroes and saviors. But all they wanted to do was rest in peace.

Cord Macklin, face as black as a thundercloud, stood over them soon after they had rolled into their blankets. He had expected only three men to return from the hills, but he had not looked for these three.

"What happened to the others?" Cord demanded, his quirt biting the dusky air.

Sherrill shook his head sadly. "Indians," he said. "They hit us this morning. We were lucky to get out alive ourselves."

Cord Macklin stood for a long moment glaring down at Sherrill. "You been lucky all the way so far, Sherrill. One o' these days your luck's goin' to run out." With a final vicious crack of his whip Cord Macklin stalked away into the gathering night.

Sherrill shifted and stretched his saddle-cramped limbs. "Cord can't understand it," he drawled. "Cord told those three to come back alone, and they didn't come back at all."

Whit Romney laughed softly. "Cord and Mitchum are liable to be lonesome the rest of the way."

CHAPTER TWELVE

The wagon train crawled on across the sun-blasted plains and undulating prairies, with the main range of the Rockies looming closer now in all its stark, lofty grandeur. There wasn't much water, perhaps barely enough, with strict rationing and luck, to carry them to the Ottaquechee. Ed Deal knew the route and was acting as scout, with Sherrill and the Romney brothers as his assistants.

Cord Macklin and Mitchum, left alone in the lead wagon, never relaxed their vigilance and never were far separated. There were men who wanted to shoot Macklin and Mitchum down like dogs, but they held back and waited on Sherrill's word. Since the excursion for water Sherry was more than ever a leader of the rank and file.

There were those, the weaker and less independent, who still clung to a kind of blind awed faith in Macklin, needing the raw brute strength of the man to bolster their own backbones. But these were fewer in number now.

Most of the hard-faced men along the line watched Macklin and Mitchum like hawks, and nerves were drawn to a thin naked edge by the tension that rode constantly with the train. Whatever else might be said about Cord and the Preacher, there was no denying their courage and fortitude. With death ever at their shoulders, they gave not the slightest evidence of cracking or crumbling.

Like everyone else, Cord Macklin knew how things were between Molley Romney and Sherrill, but he was not giving up on the girl or anything else. Confident in his own supreme power, Cord was content to wait until the time was ripe. He had long ago decided to kill Sherrill; he was certain that nothing could keep him from it. He was glad, in a way, that Sherrill had returned from the expedition for water. Cord Macklin wanted Sherrill for himself, in his own time and way. Perhaps the whip first, then the bare hands. Or a gun, if it had to be that fast.... Not many people appreciated the skill and speed that Cord Macklin had with a six-gun.

Macklin's previous position, with four trained killers at his command, had been quite secure. Now, with only Mitchum left, it was precarious at best. Fortunately for him the solemn Preacher was by far the most fearless, expert and accomplished of the lot. If the other three had been much, Sherrill and the Romney boys couldn't have wiped them out that way. Macklin was rather disappointed in Spicer. Sherrill must have been pretty sharp, or else just plain lucky. Of course Macklin was aware that Sherrill had developed considerably since joining the emigrants.

It was true. Sherrill had grown stronger and surer and better balanced on the trail, tough and lithe as whipthong. A new maturity was etched in his lean, sunburned face; the amber eyes were clear and calm and keen. He was in the saddle from sunrise to dark, a fine figure on that magnificent sorrel stallion. He and Big Red looked as if they belonged together.... Sherrill had little time for Molly Romney these days, but they could convey a lot to one another in a few words, a smile, the pressure of their hands.

They made the Ottaquechee as their water supply was becoming exhausted. The stream ran wide and full, a beautiful sight in the graying light of evening. They wheeled the lumbering wagons carefully into a tight circle, opened slightly at the river bank. It was here that the Cheyennes and Sioux had destroyed the Selway train three years ago. So far on this journey, although four lives were charged to the savages, not an Indian had been seen. But they might strike at any moment with terrifying suddenness. The guards would be doubled tonight and hereafter. Ed Deal had seen nothing, but said he was beginning to smell the bloody Cheyenne and Apaches.

After supper Sherrill and Molly sat on the river bank watching the smooth silver sheen of the Ottaquechee while darkness thickened and closed in.

"We follow this for miles now, Ed says," Sherrill told her. "All the way into the mountains. There'll be plenty of water, Molly."

"It's lovely," the girl murmured. "I never appreciated water before. There were all kinds of lakes and rivers around home, too. But you have to cross a burning desert before you know what water means."

"Yes," said Sherrill. "You learn a lot of things out here."

"I know, Sherry. It has been good for you, hasn't it?"

"The best thing that ever happened to me," he said gravely. "Harry Connover was right, Molly. I'll have to thank him sometime for having me hit over the head."

In the morning the wagon train rumbled on along the river in sun and wind and blowing dirt. Now that the Ottaquechee was always in sight, the pioneers felt better, although the towering barrier of the Rockies was forbidding and monstrous in their path. Ed Deal cheered them by reporting that the pass through here wasn't bad, easier in fact than the pass on the main Salt Lake Trail.

There were the usual incidents that delayed progress and fretted raw nerves. Wagons broke down, horses went lame, drivers fell sick, and one night a thunderstorm stampeded the cattle and it took all the next day to round them up. But on the whole things went well, the Indians did not come, and there was nothing really serious.

They rolled into the foothills and started climbing gradually, the sheer craggy heights overhanging and dwarfing them to insignificance. The Rockies looked steep and solid, utterly impassable and insurmountable, thrusting their naked peaks, spires and domes into the very clouds. It seemed incredible that humans could conquer those awesome heights, but the passage kept winding and opening before them as they climbed from hardwood timber to the somber density of pines, and labored on past the wind-twisted sentinels of the timberline to clatter through corridors of bare weathered stone.

It was no easy ascent, and progress was pathetically slow and laborious, but it was easier than it had looked from below. They crossed the crest at length and started down the western slope, the horses and other draft animals snorting and bracing back, brakes screaming and smoking, men hurrying back and forth along the row to help where it was needed. It was a battle all the way, and they fought it tooth and claw with everything in them, swearing or praying through clenched teeth as they worked with raw bleeding hands, blocking wheels, holding panicky horses, righting tipped wagons, braking with man-power when the mechanical brakes failed.

At last they hit the bottom and it was all over. They made camp in the western foothills, and exhausted men slept for ten or twelve hours without a break. Getting up late the next morning, they looked back at the mountains and shook their heads in wonder. They had done it.

Rested, the emigrants picked up the course of the Onion River and wound their way northwest toward Fort Bridger. The worst was behind them now, they thought, and this was the beginning of the home stretch. Spirits rose accordingly and there was better feeling along the wagons, a cheerful optimism prevailed. They were going through; they were going to make it. Before too long they'd be hauling into Bridger.

One night there was a festive atmosphere in the camp. Everybody had bathed in the river, the women and men in relays, and changed into clean clothing. "Saturday night," someone said, and the word spread like magic. "It's Saturday night and we ought to celebrate. Put that side of beef on the fire, and drag out that little old jug. Get the fiddle and guitar, the accordion and mouth-organ, and let's have some music here. It's Saturday night on the Onion River!"

The gaiety grew of itself, spontaneous and highly contagious, sweeping from campfire to fire with laughter and chatter and song. Whiskey jugs appeared and beer kegs were tapped while the beefs were roasting. Men stood in merry, boisterous groups as the liquor went around, and in the wagons young girls hunted for their best bright dresses. Children raced and romped about the oval, and music started up here and there in the early twilight.

After everyone had drunk and feasted well, the women cleaned up while the men lounged back with pipes, cigars and cigarettes to smoke and talk. Later an orchestra was formed to play for dancing, and old and young alike swung joyously into it, with fat Ed Deal singing and calling the square dances.

Mrs. Romney, still graceful and light on her feet, danced with Jud and Whit after failing to persuade her husband to try it, and her flushed, laughing face looked nearly as young as Molly's in the flickering firelight. Everybody was dancing, it seemed, even the young Potter widow, and Sherrill finally let Molly draw him into it.

"I'm bad enough on a smooth floor," he protested.

But Molly was insistent, and after a few minutes they were dancing very well together, and the women were remarking what a fine handsome couple they made as they stepped daintily to the strains of the song Ed Deal was singing: *"Put your little foot, put your little foot, put your little foot right out...."*

When Cord Macklin came to claim his number with Molly, Sherrill faced him briefly, stark hatred between them, and hundreds of eyes were on them. But nothing happened. Cord led Molly away, and Sherrill walked to the wagon wheel where Whit and Jud were leaning with a jug, lifted the jug and took a deep swig.

"Ah, I needed that," Sherrill said. "Dancing gives me a thirst."

"A thirsty business," agreed Jud. "And a dull one."

Sherrill danced once with Mrs. Romney, visited the boys and their jug again, and went out to relieve Ferris on guard duty.

"You don't have to do this, Sherry," said Ferris. "It's my watch."

"Go on; get a drink and a dance," Sherrill said. "I've had enough of it."

"I'm sure obliged, Sherry," said Ferris, grinning and hastening toward the circle, where Ed Deal was singing the sad, haunting refrain of *Red River Valley*. Ferris was looking for pretty Mrs. Potter.

Cord Macklin asked Molly to walk down by the river, but she declined with firm politeness. When the music stopped she left him and went to her brothers, then passed on to find the sentry post Sherrill had taken over. Cord Macklin stood with hands on hips staring after the girl, his black eyes shining and his lips compressed. He strode to the sideline, where Mitchum was gloomily cradling a jug of whiskey, and picked up his quirt.

"Don't drink too much o' that rotgut," Macklin warned.

"I never have yet," said Mitchum. "Don't reckon I'll start here. You cut a real neat figure, Cord."

Macklin peered narrowly at him, lashed up dust with the quirt, and paced restlessly away. Mitchum up-ended the jug over his forearm and gulped generously. All liquor did to him was increase his natural melancholy.

Molly came upon Sherrill gazing out over the moonlit prairie. "Didn't you like the dance, Sherry?" she asked.

"Yes, it's good to see people happy," he said. "They deserve it. And they need it, too."

"And you don't?"

Sherrill studied her gravely. "I need it as much as anybody— maybe more. About the only kind I ever knew came out of a bottle."

Molly Romney raised her face. "Why don't you take it then?"

"I've got some things to do—first."

"Well," she smiled, "you could at least take a sample."

Sherrill laughed and caught her firm, slender body in his arm. "Why, you little devil," he said, bending his head over her eager, radiant face.

CHAPTER THIRTEEN

At daybreak the Indians came howling down out of the foot-hills to attack the encampment that was sleeping off its night of revelry. The emigrants wakened to the crash of rifle fire, the whine of bullets and zing of arrows, the weird unearthly war cries of the charging savages.

Men threshed and kicked out of their blankets and groped for gun belts and carbines, groaning and sick from the after-effects of liquor, cursing and swearing as they stumbled and plunged to their places under and between the wagons or behind the wheels.

"What a mornin' for 'em to come!" they grumbled disgust-edly, kneeling, crouching, or lying prone to draw beads on the racing ponies and half naked riders. "Don't the blasted heathens know it's Sunday?"

The first wave of warriors, yipping and yowling insanely, had hurtled in close to the ringed wagons before the defense was orga-nized, striking terror into the women and children, making the spines and scalps of the men tingle and crawl. But now the pio-neer rifles were hammering away steadily, mowing them down in long ragged windrows, breaking and scattering the assault, driv-ing the redskins back. One reckless brave catapulted his pony between two wagons into the enclosure, and died instantly there with a dozen bullets in his body. But the others had withdrawn hastily to a safe distance, leaving dead and wounded Indians and horses strewn about the plain.

"Cheyennes," said Ed Deal. "There ain't enough of 'em to hit a train this size. If they caught us strung out on the trail they might do some damage, but this way they can't hurt us none. Tell your womenfolks and kids not to worry. You boys that need a drink to steady yuh, grab a quick one before they come back—if they come."

The Indians, by no means anxious to come back into that deadly withering blast, contented themselves mainly with dashing back and forth in wide arcs, putting on a long-range show of horsemanship accompanied by hideous howling and ineffectual volleys of arrows and shots. Occasionally some of the more foolhardy bucks raced in closer to the circle of wagons and died screeching in the dust as they were picked off by expert marksmen. But most of the braves performed their wild antics at a respectable distance.

"The foolish young bucks!" snorted Ed Deal. "They don't wanta fight; they just wanta show off and holler."

The women had overcome their first panic and were busy calming the children and one another. The Cheyennes, after that first mad rush, did not seem exceptionally warlike. Here and there one of them whooped himself into a frenzy and made a suicidal solo flight toward the wagons. Sherrill lined his Henry rifle on the brown body of one of these in-driving maniacs, firing twice to drop him in a spectacular flying fall to the sand.

"Well, there's my first Indian," Sherrill said to nobody in particular.

Whit Romney shook his blond head. "I haven't hit one of 'em yet."

Molly Romney frowned. "You talk as if you were at target practice."

"About what it amounts to," said Jud, scowling along his rifle barrel. "I think I winged that one with the red band on his head."

A score or more of the brown-skinned corpses were sprawled on the reddish dirt and the bleached bunch-grass of the prairie. A woman screamed as the painted body nearest the wagon ring came to sudden life, leaping forward and waving a tomahawk, daubed face horribly distorted. Mitchum, standing nearby, nonchalantly pulled a six-shooter and plugged the charging brave, who pitched headlong into the shadow of the wagons.

"They're crazy," Sherrill said. "They don't make sense."

Whit Romney nudged him, grinning. "There, I got one, Sherry! See him flopping around out there?"

The Cheyennes tried one more mass attack, streaming in with fanatical fury, and for a few minutes things were very hot along the barricades. A bullet whisked Sherrill's hat off, an arrow nailed Jud's sleeve to the tailboard, and a lance slithered off the spokes of the wheel Whit was crouching behind. Several of the madmen thundered right into the wagon-sides before the bullets caught and riddled them. Mr. Romney shot one buck right off the tongue of the Conestoga.

The surviving braves broke into flight once more, and this time they stayed back out of range, cavorting to and fro on their ponies. Apparently the Cheyennes had tired of this costly and futile demonstration against the wagon train. After a short council of war, or peace, they loosed a final barrage of shots, arrows and defiant cries, and went yipping off into the low-lying foothills on the north.

In the circle of wagons they checked for casualties. Ferris, on sentry duty again that morning, had been killed in the first onslaught, and a man named Vreeland died in repulsing the final assault. Outside of that, there was no loss of life except for one horse, a mule, and two steers. Chaffee had his arm broken by a bullet, Duval was wounded in the thigh, and a woman had been scratched by a spent arrow. That was all, and even the kids were scornful of the Indian warriors, now that their initial fright had passed and the redskins were gone.

Ed Deal regarded the capers of the children and the levity of some adults with somber disapproval. "If the Cheyennes come back in force it ain't goin' to be funny," Ed said. "Don't think for a minute they can't fight. Don't think they wouldn't overrun this camp if they was enough of 'em."

"Let's bury the dead and get movin'," Cord Macklin said callously. "Them Indians won't be back."

"No," Ed Deal said flatly. "We'll wait a spell. They'd cut us to pieces on the road."

Cord Macklin perceived that the ranks were solidly behind Ed Deal, and for the first time Macklin allowed his authority to be overruled, shrugging his powerful shoulders and walking off without an argument.

Men were already digging two graves in the oval, and now that there was time they decided to hold burial services. Vreeland left a wife, four teen-age children, and an aged mother. Ferris, young, unmarried, and well liked on the train, had been traveling with his parents and sister. Recently Ferris had shown a warm interest in the attractive young Potter widow, which was one reason Sherrill had freed him from guard duty last night during the dance. Alone with her baby, she would need another husband out here, and Ferris would have made her a good one.

Mrs. Potter did not attend the ceremonies. Ed Deal's wife remained in the wagon with her, and Ed's eyes strayed in that direction from time to time. "Pure unlucky, that girl," whispered Ed Deal. "One o' them nice kinda people that always gets tromped on and kicked around."

They waited three hours before breaking the ring and forming for the trail. The Indians did not return that morning. They had had their excitement, lost a third of their party and retired, possibly to lick their wounds and recruit a stronger force for the next attempt.... The heavy wagons lurched and creaked into line and rolled on beside the Onion River toward Fort Bridger.

Days passed and there were no more Indians, no more delays. Sherrill thought: *Macklin must be starting to worry some about this time....* It looked as if the train would go through in spite of Macklin and Mitchum, and in back of them Lilli Lavery.

Nothing had been able to stop it thus far. Not the South Branch, the lack of water, the suffering and deaths from illness, the Rocky Mountains, the murder of Wilson, Potter and McLowry, or the Cheyennes. Nothing could stop it now unless the Indians attacked in such overwhelming numbers as to destroy the train. Macklin must be doing a lot of tall thinking these days and nights. He must be getting desperate, but he still gave no sign of cracking under the pressure. Whatever his faults, Cord Macklin was a man of iron.

Sherrill was awakened one morning early, before sunup, by someone tugging at his blankets. Turning over in sleepy protest, he saw Ed Deal's thin, spinsterish wife crouching there with an anxious look on her bony countenance.

"Ed didn't come in last night," she said. "He was on late sentry, but he ought to be in bed before now. I'm worried, Mr. Sherry. I got a feelin' somethin's gone wrong."

"You go back to bed, Mrs. Deal," said Sherrill. "I'll get the boys up and we'll take a look around. Don't worry about Ed. He's probably still on watch somewhere."

Sherrill roused the Romney brothers and they made a tour of the circuit. None of the sentries had seen Ed for several hours, but they were positive he must be in camp some place. They halted at the corral near the lead wagon and spotted Ed's big gray gelding among the other horses.

"But I don't see Macklin's horse—or Mitchum's," Sherrill said after a thorough inspection.

There were no signs of life around the lead wagon, either. They shouted and pounded on the sides, but there was no response. Finally, with drawn guns, they climbed in to search the huge wagon. Sherrill was afraid of what they might discover before they even started. His fears increased as he observed an erratic streak of dark stains across the bales and bundles in the rear of the wagon. Ed Deal's corpulent form lay under a tarpaulin in one corner in a dry-crusted black pool of blood. The mark of the whip striped his broad face, and there were three knife wounds in his wide back, any one of which would have been fatal.

"Another for Macklin," Sherrill gritted through his teeth. "Cord lashed him blind with the quirt and Mitchum put the steel into his back. I should've killed those two long before this.... Boys, let's not say anything about this right away."

They clambered out, sick and desolate, and walked back to the Romney wagon in silence, remembering how jolly Ed Deal had been the night of the dance, jigging and shaking as he chanted out the numbers, beaming happily at everybody, hoisting a jug with a look of rapture on his fat, rosy, sweating face. And singing: *"Put your arm around, put your arm around, put your arm around her waist...."* Everyone had loved Ed Deal.

Mr. Romney, his grave, lined face stricken and aged, lowered himself stiffly from the Conestoga as the boys approached. "Where's Molly?" he asked brokenly. "Have you seen Molly?"

They stared at him, bewildered, unbelieving and aghast, trying to hide their fear and dread.

Sherrill said quickly: "Maybe she got up early to walk by the river. She likes it there."

But he knew he lied. She was with Macklin and Mitchum, who had taken her somehow in the night, and Ed Deal was dead because he had tried to stop them. Whit and Jud knew it, too, but they didn't know how to tell their father.

Mr. Romney shook his head. "No. I woke up in the night and felt something wrong. But I was tired, I went back to sleep.... She's gone, I know she's gone."

"Yes, Mr. Romney," Sherrill said evenly. "Macklin and Mitchum are gone, too, and they must have taken Molly with them. Ed Deal tried to prevent it and they killed him; we just found Ed's body in the lead wagon. But they won't harm Molly; she'll be all right. I'm going after her now."

"But *where* would they take her?" asked Mr. Romney. "And why?"

"Fort Bridger," Sherrill said. "Macklin wants to marry her. But he never will, I'll see to that. Whit, will you put my saddle on Red?"

"You can't go alone, Sherry," protested Whit. "I'm going with you."

"No, Whit, you're needed more right here. You and Jud will have to bring the train in."

"I'll get Big Red for you, Sherry," Jud said, heading for the rear remuda.

Sherrill shifted his gun belt, checked the .44 Colts, and examined the Henry rifle. Mr. Romney was preparing some foodstuff for the saddle bags, and the young Potter widow appeared surprisingly with a pot of hot coffee.

Whit was still arguing. "But, Sherry, there's two of *them!*"

"The two I want, kid," said Sherrill. "I'll take care of them. These people here need you, Whit. I'll go get Molly, and you Romneys get the wagons in." He bowed gratefully to Mrs. Potter and gulped the strong coffee.

Jud came back with the horse saddled, and Sherrill stroked Big Red's proud arched neck while Mr. Romney stuffed food into the saddle bags. Jud filled two canteens with fresh water. Whit was rolling Sherrill's blankets, and as he went to strap the roll on behind the saddle Sherry slung on an extra belt of .44 caliber ammunition, which could be used in the Henry as well as the revolver.

"Don't worry now," Sherrill said. "Macklin won't hurt Molly, or let anybody else hurt her. You folks bring the wagons in. I'll send the cavalry out to meet you, if I can."

"God bless you, boy," murmured Mr. Romney.

"I'll get Molly for you," Sherrill promised.

"Take me with you, Sherry," pleaded Whit, his gray eyes almost tearful.

But Sherrill was already stepping into the saddle.

"You've got your job to do here, Whit," he said gently. "This is mine—all mine."

CHAPTER FOURTEEN

Sherrill stayed hard on the trail all through that burning day, but even with a horse like Big Red it was a two days' ride into Fort Bridger. He was constantly on the alert against ambush, aware that Mitchum might have been left behind to check any pursuit, but he saw nothing except gophers, prairie dogs, coyotes, jackrabbits, and the whitened bones that marked the route all the way from the Mississippi. If Macklin's party had pushed right through they would get into town tonight, he surmised. They must have gone to Bridger; there was no other place in the vicinity to go. Salt Lake City was still too far away for them to attempt.

Sherrill wondered at the daring of two men cutting straight through the heart of the Cheyenne country with a girl prisoner on their hands. Then he recalled something he had heard about Mitchum back in Bedloe Landing, to the effect that the Preacher had been out west with the Mormons and knew the Indians, particularly the Cheyennes; that he spoke and understood their language. If that were the case, they had little or nothing to fear from the red-men. In fact, they might even visit the savages and incite them to assault the wagon train. Sherrill went cold all over at the thought. Perhaps it had been part of the Lavery scheme from the first, a final resort if the column got this close to Fort Bridger.

He rode the sun out of sight behind the western horizon. Man and mount were worn, weary, dust-plastered and sun-dazed when darkness overtook them. There was nothing to do but bed down in the open. It would be cold in the night without a fire, but Sherrill dared not light one.

While Big Red drank and cooled off in the Onion River, Sherrill chewed the dry roast beef and biscuits, washing it down with water. Selecting a spot in the shelter of a boulder, he bedded Big Red down and curled up in his blankets close to the warmth of the great stallion. But there was too much on Sherrill's mind to permit him to fall asleep at once.

He should have killed Macklin and Mitchum before it came to this. It would have been infinitely better for all concerned if he had shot Macklin back at the Landing. That had been his impulse, of course, but at the time reason had seemed to dictate otherwise. Ironically, as it was later revealed, Cord Macklin had been deemed indispensable to the wagon train.

He thought of all the people who would still be alive if he had eliminated Macklin and his lieutenants in the beginning: the whole Wilson family, Potter, McLowry, Ed Deal, and the old folks and kids who had perished on the South Branch. Possibly Ferris and Vreeland, too .... Well, it was a mistake that could not be remedied, an error in judgment that no one could be rightly blamed for. The only payment left to exact lay in the lives of Cord Macklin and Preacher Mitchum. Sherrill intended to collect hat, even if it meant forfeiting his own life in exchange.

Sherrill was less worried about Molly Romney than might have been expected, figuring that Macklin valued the girl too highly to mistreat her in any way. Macklin, seeing that the train was going through and that Molly was lost to him, had resorted to this final flagrant ruse. It was a desperate measure, a drastic last effort that was no more than an admission of defeat.

Macklin would undoubtedly try to force Molly into marriage. If that failed, he was likely to revert to the brutal tactics he had employed with Veronica Patchin .... Fury flared up in Sherrill like a torch at white heat. He would get there before that stage was reached, even if he had to ride Big Red to death under him.... He thought of how it would feel to get Cord Macklin under his guns after all these months and miles.

Sherrill was back in the saddle before daylight, chilled and cramped and sore, turning Big Red upgrade as the trail diverged from the river to climb and cross a high, barren plateau, shadowed at intervals by clustered stone spires and columns, irregular buttes and domes of red and ocher rock. It was a fantastic country, sun-struck, tortured, grotesquely beautiful, flaming with the violent colors of weird rock formations thrusting angularly skyward.

The sun soared and blazed in a molten sky, climbing steadily to its midday zenith, reflected dazzlingly from the rock surfaces on every side, the heat beating down and rising again from the hard, blistered earth. Occasional breezes fanned from the canyons and dry arroyos with a furnace breath. Horse and rider were soaked with sweat and smeared with dust. Now and then they paused in the shade of stone pillars, for Sherrill to drink from a canteen and water Big Red from his hat.

It was afternoon when Sherrill sensed danger. He was still on the broad, high tableland, cut with dry gulches and ravines, ridged on the north, the river lying somewhere to the south. He scanned the scorched landscape with vigilance and saw nothing, but the feeling of being watched persisted.

The fort could not be too many miles ahead now. Big Red had been making time, but Sherrill held him in here and proceeded with wary alertness, every instinct sharpened by his promonition of menacing trouble. Somebody was watching him from some concealed vantage point; he would have sworn to it. He could feel the eyes upon him, and his spine prickled coldly under the sweat as he waited for the threat to come out in the open, his scalp creeping and bristling.

When it came it was almost a relief. Sudden as a desert mirage, the Indians appeared on the distant skyline of a northern ridge, and then the bare slope was blurred and darkened as they poured down toward him on their fleet ponies, their cries floating thin and shrill on the heat-laden air. It was a larger force than had attacked the emigrants' camp; there were hundreds of them this time.

Panic fluttered up in Sherrill and frayed out thinly before the stronger blade of his disgust. *What luck!* he thought bitterly. *What awful luck....* To have them come now when he was almost in, when he was so near to Fort Bridger and the end of a thousand-mile trail. Just as he was about to catch up with Cord Macklin and Mitchum.... He wondered if Mitchum had contrived this uprising. There were enough braves in this band to wipe out that column of wagons.

Lifting the Henry rifle from its boot, Sherrill laid the butt firmly against his right shoulder, sighted, squeezed the trigger, and saw the foremost pony cartwheel over into a dust cloud at the bottom of the ridge. Under him, Big Red stood steady and solid, unshaken and calm. Sherrill lined his sights on another bobbing figure, elevated a trifle, and fired again to spill the second horse and rider.

But the others came on in a hideous red horde, unhesitating and sure of their quarry. Sherrill wheeled the red stallion and started his run for the river. It was the only chance and a very slight one. Big Red could outrun and outlast any of those Indian ponies—but not forever. Sherrill was caught in the middle of nowhere with only the river to head for.

From this plateau there must be bluffs dropping sharply to the Onion. If he hit them right he might get away, because there was no jump he wouldn't try in this predicament. When the redskins got a lone rider, they preferred to take him alive and torture him. This habit of theirs might prove his salvation. At any rate, he wouldn't be taken alive. His teeth tightened until his jaws ached up into his ears. He *wouldn't be taken at all.*

He couldn't be; he had to get away. He had to rescue Molly Romney and turn his guns loose on Mitchum and Macklin. He must live long enough, at least, to see Cord Macklin dead. Not only for Patch but for himself, for the Wilsons and Potter, for McLowry and Ed Deal and all the rest.... His teeth grated as he thought of Lilli Lavery, the fiendish female who was behind all this. He was convinced now that Mitchum and Macklin had roused the Cheyennes to set them on him and the wagon train.

They were spreading behind him now, fanning out east and west so that he couldn't turn if he wanted to. It had to be the river. The shots they sent after him were mostly wild. They couldn't shoot anyway, but the idea was they wanted him alive. They wanted him roasting in a slow fire to pay for those young bucks who had thrown their lives away against the encircled wagons.

They were in no hurry, certain of their victim, knowing they would hem him in at the river. Sherrill swiveled in the saddle and fired the Henry, missed, tried again and failed, but it helped slow the chase. Sherrill went back to his riding and the powerful stallion surged ahead with even greater speed. He could outrace them, he was gaining all the time, but there was nowhere to go, no way out of the trap except the Onion River. A hundred-foot cliff was what he wanted. *I'll take it,* Sherrill thought. *No matter how high. I'll take it and they won't.*

The table-top dipped now, but the river was not in view. That meant a long, steep drop, thank goodness. If only it were sheer about the water.... He was thundering closer in mighty reaching strides, the dust smoking up in back of him, Big Red magnificent and indomitable between his gripping thighs. Ahead and far below he saw the cottonwoods that strung along the river valley. It was going to be high all right, if only the river wasn't too distant. Bullets burred and hummed overhead, arrows swished and lifted the dirt, and savage screams split the sunlight as the Indians pressed in along the plateau.

He was near, very near the chasm now, and Big Red was trying to veer away, but Sherrill held him straight on toward the edge of the bluff, held him and drove him full tilt and straightaway.

They hurtled on, and the rim looked sharp as the edge of a knife. The southern flats beyond the river were visible, but in between there was nothing yet but open space. It would be high and steep enough, *but how far from the water?* Big Red was pulling away now and Sherrill could not hold him; the horse was pulling Sherrill's arms out of their sockets. They slid to a plunging, rearing stop on the brink of the precipice. The horse wouldn't take it.

"I don't blame you, boy," Sherrill said. "I don't blame you a bit."

He swung from the saddle, swearing softly and gauging his distances. It was a sheer drop of maybe fifty feet. The Onion River looked directly below, but there was a boulder-piled bank that had to be cleared. It would take a great leap; it would be a close thing.

"Run for it, Red," Sherrill said. "Show those Indians how a real horse runs." He pointed east in the direction of the wagon train and slapped Big Red smartly on the flank.

The stallion reared and neighed in protest, pawed the ground and tried to nuzzle Sherrill. He smacked the glistening wet red flank once more, and Bid Red bounded off and stretched forward into his beautiful flowing stride. Sherrill snarled out an involuntary protest as one of the warriors pulled over near the path of the sorrel's flight and deliberately drove his lance deep into Big Red's side. The horse was still screaming in the death throes when Sherrill's swift shot knocked the lance-thrower spinning from his pony.

Sherrill swerved around to face the oncoming Indians. Shots droned and arrows swooshed, stone fragments and dirt pelted him, but they weren't really trying for the kill yet. "Come on, you red buzzards!" Sherry yelled, raising the Henry and firing rapidly, blowing another brave off his bareback perch, bringing down two more ponies with their riders in the weltering dust.

Still they wavered and loitered, taunting and mocking him, biding their time in jockeying to and fro. Except for one painted madman who charged in on foot and hurled a spear that Sherrill barely dodged. Sherrill shot down the spearman and threw the empty rifle over the cliff to keep it from their hands.

Still on fire over the useless wanton slaying of Big Red, Sherrill ripped out his two six-guns and stalked toward the Cheyennes, shooting with steady precision, ablaze with hatred for the brutal clay-daubed creatures. Picking them off, making every shot count, Sherrill triggered until both hammers clicked on empty shells. A lone rider streaked in and dived insanely from his mount at Sherrill. Pivoting away, Sherrill smashed that shaven skull with his right-hand gun and turned to the river, flipping both Colt .44's over the rim with keen regret, unbuckling and dropping his cartridge belt.

Measuring the take-off, Sherrill broke into a run under a storm of arrows and bullets. Driving hard with his legs, he leaped out with every atom of power in his body, flinging himself high and far from the top of the bluff. There was a wild defiant exultance in him as he flew off into space, hearing the angry thwarted shouts behind him through the rush of air.

For an instant he seemed to hang suspended in emptiness. Then he was falling, toppling from the peak of his jump, still straining outward to clear those cruel rocks at the bottom. Sherrill tried to hold his balance, but he was turning as he fell, somersaulting and twisting, the sun and earth and water whirling crazily about him. He was dropping faster now in a sickening rush, breathless but still fighting, plunging down toward destruction.

Jagged out-thrusting rocks flashed by his blurred eyes, he glimpsed clear water underneath, and then the water smashed him, solid as concrete, beating the last breath from his lungs and the light from his vision. The cold depths revived him and he struggled upward against the undertow of the current, bumping a slimy boulder, working numb arms and legs in a frenzy. It seemed a long way, an endless time. His skull was bursting when he broke the surface and gulped air hungrily, dully amazed at finding himself still alive.

Only half conscious, Sherrill drifted downstream, straining feebly to keep his face above water, jarred by contacts with rocks and driftwood. Bullets and arrows were splashing and churning the river around him, and once his head cleared somewhat he submerged for safety's sake. Surfacing again, he saw the sky blackened by the hurtling downward rush of bodies, pony and Indian screeching as they crashed to their death on a stone-girded shelf at the base of the cliff. Sherrill ducked under and swam with the tide. Emerging once more, he lay back in utter weariness and let the current carry him.

They were still shooting from above, but their aim was poor. After that one fatal attempt nobody else cared to try the leap. The high bluff ran for miles along the Onion River; there was no way for them to get down after him. He had been fortunate all right; his luck was in again. He had been spared to save Molly Romney and take vengeance on Cord Macklin and Preacher Mitchum. Sherrill smiled faintly and let himself float with the flowing stream.

The Cheyennes, cheated of one victim, would go after the wagon train now crazed with the blood-lust. Sherrill hoped the pioneers would have time to form a circle for defense. If they got into a ring they might be able to beat off the Indians until reinforcements arrived from Fort Bridger.

When Sherrill felt strong enough he started swimming for the low opposite bank, weighed down by his boots and clothes, making slow, laborious progress. Crawling out on the pebbled shore, he clambered for cover and stretched out in exhaustion to let the hot sun dry his clothing and body. He had lost about everything but his life. Without Big Red and his guns, he felt naked, alone and helpless. His hat was gone, too, of course, leaving him vulnerable to sunstroke.

It must be ten or fifteen miles yet into Bridger, perhaps more, a terrible hike under the pitiless glare of the afternoon sun. Well, he'd just have to plug along and make it somehow.... But first he'd get dried out and rested.

Sherrill felt badly about Big Red and he missed the Colt .44's he had worn so long and constantly, the guns that should have killed Macklin and Mitchum. But then, he supposed any guns would do, and it didn't matter as long as those two men died.... Sherrill had dismissed the Indians for the time being. He was thinking of Cord Macklin and Mitchum now.

Two hours later, reeling through shimmering heat along the river side with a wet scarf tied about his head, Sherrill was talking to himself and seeing all manner of extravagant fantasies on the burning plain. That squad of blue-uniformed troopers from Fort Bridger was another mirage, and Sherrill refused to look at them after the first glance, until they were all around him and he could smell the sweat of horses and men and the hot leather in the sunshine. And a well remembered voice saying, with deep emotion: *"Sherry! For heaven's sake, Sherry!..."* He looked up then and saw the familiar square, sober face, and his eyes filled with sudden tears as he tried to smile.

It was Sergeant Steve Ehlers, who had known Sherrill and Patchin, and later McLowry, in the old devil-may-care days back in Memphis, Natchez, and New Orleans. Sergeant Ehlers, in command of a small detachment from the fort.

CHAPTER FIFTEEN

As the following afternoon waned Sherrill sat on a bunk in the C Company barracks at Fort Bridger, with Sergeant Steve Ehlers lounging on the next bed. Sherrill had eaten and slept well, bathed in warm water for the first time in months, had a shave and haircut from the company barber, and was feeling clean and fine, refreshed and comfortable, nagged only by his impatience. He wore borrowed underclothes and levis, an old army shirt, faded but newly laundered, and he told Ehlers he felt all dressed up and ready to do the town.

The Sergeant had also dug out for him an old double-holstered gun belt with a pair of Colt .44's. After cleaning and oiling the weapons with infinite care, they had gone to the range so Sherrill could try the guns, get the heft and feel and balance of them, familiarize himself with the trigger-pull and recoil. Back in the barracks he still wore the belt, and frequently eased the guns out and into the sheaths, practicing his draw with the strange equipment.

A troop of cavalry had set forth last night to meet the wagon train on the Onion River, and Sherrill's mind was relieved on that score. The major had cursed and grumbled at first about having to patrol half the entire West with a handful of men, and then had elected to lead the expedition himself.

"Don't understand what got the Cheyennes up all at once," the major had muttered with a frown. "They haven't given us any trouble for some time."

"There's a renegade from the train who might have had something to do with it, Major," Sherrill told him.

"One of those men who came into town with the girl? I'll attend to him when I return, Mr. Sherrill."

Sherrill had smiled gravely. "I doubt if he'll be around when you get back, Major."

"What? Well, I could send a detail after him right now."

"I wish you wouldn't, Major," said Sherrill. "I'd like to take care of that myself."

The major had grunted at this, "You'll see that he doesn't get away?"

"He won't get away," Sherrill said quietly.

The major had eyed him closely and nodded. "I'm inclined to believe you, my boy. Good luck to you. We'll bring in your wagons."

Now Sherrill rose and paced restlessly, drew right-and left-handed, then both hands simultaneously, and went to the mirror on the wall to study his changed face with some perplexity. It was like staring at a stranger. It was the face of a man, not the grinning devil-may-care boy's face he had seen reflected in Bedloe's Landing and previous to that. Sherrill had grown up on the trail, as Harry Connover had prophesied, and it showed plainly. The amber eyes were straight and clear and steady. There was strength and firmness about the mouth and chin. The bone structure stood out sharply under the deeply bronzed skin. Sherrill nodded solemnly at his image; he had come of age at last. He turned away with a laugh:

"You'd think I was going to a dance."

"Have you got a plan for tonight?" the sergeant asked.

Steve Ehlers knew the whole story, and had been shocked and grieved to hear about Veronica and Patch and the murder of McLowry. He was a broad, solid man, a few years older than Sherrill, with a square, rugged face, somber gray eyes, and dark hair prematurely tinged with gray. They had spent hours reliving the old happy-go-lucky days on the Mississippi, recalling with laughter one jamboree after another.

Before finding Sherrill out there beside the river, Ehlers had known that two men and a girl from some wagon train were in town. The girl, ill and worn out from her trip across the plains and mountains, had gone directly to her room in the Colorado Hotel and had not been seen since. It was rumored that she was very beautiful. The two men had been spending most of their time downstairs in the barroom, speaking to nobody but each other and the bartender.

"I don't need a plan," Sherrill answered. "It's just a matter of going in after them."

"They'll be ready," Ehlers said. "And there's two of them. It'd be better to have them arrested."

Sherrill shook his sun-streaked, reddish gold head. "They'd fight that as quick as they will me, Steve. And this is my fight. I don't think they'll be expecting me anyway. They figure my scalp is drying in a Cheyenne lodge by now."

"I know how you feel, Sherry," said Steve Ehlers. "But I don't like it. You and Patch lifted your guns a few times for me, as I recall it. I think I'll go along with you tonight."

"You don't want to lose those stripes, Sergeant."

"I won't," Ehlers said. "They're outlaws, murderers, renegades. It falls in the line of duty."

"Look, Steve," said Sherrill. "There was a boy with the train who wanted to come along. The brother of that girl and a good friend of mine. I wouldn't let him, and I can't let you. It's my play, Steve."

Ehlers smiled soberly. "All right, Sherry, you can have it. But I'll be hanging around, boy. You can't stop a soldier from having a drink or two."

"I can't figure their game yet," Sherrill confessed. "I should think they'd be hitting for Salt Lake."

"They aren't in any hurry," said Ehlers. "They're counting on the wagon train being massacred to the last man. They think they're safe enough here."

"I suppose so, Steve."

"They probably packed all the whiskey they could carry into that Cheyenne village. They must have got them started. The Indians in these parts have been peaceful and friendly, until this outbreak."

Sherrill stood up and slapped the sheathed guns. "I'm going in and get it done with."

Ehlers got up and gripped Sherry's shoulders. "Wait, boy, wait a little. No sense getting shot down without even seeing them. When it's dark we'll ride to town in the back of a wagon. You've got to get in close before they spot you, Sherry."

"What if they pull out?"

"They aren't leaving," Ehlers said. "My little waitress friend says they can't get the girl out of that room."

"Macklin won't fool around like that forever."

"He don't have to. Just till tonight."

Sherrill relaxed and smiled thinly. "All right, Steve, we'll wait. I could clean and oil these guns again. Can't waste any more shells on the range. Or do you want to play a little poker?"

Sergeant Ehlers spread his wide palms and grinned. "Not with you, not for money. I saw enough of your poker playing back on the Mississippi." He fumbled in his blouse for pencil and paper. "I'll diagram the ground floor of the Colorado Hotel for you. It'll help to have some idea of the layout."

Ehlers sketched swiftly, neatly and concisely. "Here's the front entrance to the lobby, the desk here, the stairs going up here. To the right off the foot of the stairs a broad open doorway goes into the saloon. A side door here opens from the barroom into an alley...." Sherrill watched and remembered the maps of McLowry, and was lonesome again for the tough little one-eyed scout.

Sherrill shaped a cigarette and thought of Molly Romney locked in a bare, cheerless room of that hotel, and her family worrying themselves sick out there with the wagons, unless they were too busy fighting for their lives to think about anything else.... His mind went back to Bedloe Landing and wise, polished Harry Connover, haughty Jay Lavery dying under Jud's gun barrel, the evil loveliness of Lilli, Dakin dead in a dark gutter, Nina Montez with her quaint accented voice, Patchin lying blind and lonely in the Queen's Hotel.

He thought of the long trail, brawling with Big Jess outside the Ox-Bow in Independence, the dispute at the fork and the theatrical appearance of Holway and Mitchum. The Wilson family annihilated, Potter shot in the back, Mc Lowry with his head bashed in and the scalplock gone, fat Ed Deal whiplashed and stabbed.... He saw again three men dying suddenly in the firelit woods—Spicer, Holway and Koogle—all richly deserving their fate. He saw Big Red rearing high with that Cheyenne lance shivering in his shining side.

Sherrill strode to a window and stared out over the empty parade ground of officers' row and the stockade wall.

"Will night ever come?" he murmured irritably.

"It'll come," Ehlers said. "After waiting this long, Sherry, you shouldn't mind a few hours."

"That's the trouble, Steve—I've waited too all-fired long," said Sherrill. "Where are those old gloves with the stout leather cuffs? I'm going to need those cuffs if I want to have any hands left on me."

Steve Ehlers found the gloves and started sawing off the cuffs with a hunting knife. Sherrill watched the operation intently through a haze of tobacco smoke. The minutes ticked past with excruciating slowness.

Night did come, after an eternity of waiting. In the hooded rear of a supply wagon, they bumped and clattered from the stockaded fort into the single street of the rude frontier settlement at the river bend. Sherrill had the leather cuffs taped on his wrists under the faded blue shirtsleeves. They were flexible enough not to interfere with his wrist action, and they would offer some protection against Cord Macklin's quirt. Neither Sherrill nor Ehlers spoke on the way into town. The driver was whistling *The Battle Cry of Freedom,* and it rasped unbearably on Sherrill's raw nerves.

Sherrill's thoughts were with the wagon train. The Indians would have struck this morning; the battle on the Onion River must be over before now. He hoped and prayed that the cavalry had reached there in time.... He visualized again the clear, pleasant faces of the Romney family in the campfire glow, saw Mrs. Romney laughing as she danced with her fine tall sons, and he thought of Molly with an intolerable aching tenderness and yearning. The Romneys were the finest folks he had ever known, outside of his own family. Odd that they should be Yankees from one of the most radically Abolitionist states in the North.

The wagon turned and rattled into the alley beside the Colorado Hotel. Sergeant Ehlers restrained Sherrill. "Wait here a minute while I look around." He swung over the tailboard and walked away.

Sherrill stood up in under the canvas and moved his arms and legs to keep them loose and limber. He had to be right tonight; he had to be better than ever before. He had seen Mitchum in Bedloe Landing. The Preacher was inhumanly cool and sure, fast and deadly, absolutely without fear. And Cord Macklin, of course, would be terrible to face.... But Sherrill was ready. He felt fresh and strong and supple, his muscles alive and rippling responsively, his mind alert and keen, his eyes quick and sharp.

Steve Ehlers came back and leaned casually on the tailboard smoking a cigar, while Sherrill crouched close to hear his words.

"They're still here but I didn't see 'em. They've been acting kind of nervous and jumpy since the troops went out last night. Macklin's up in his room now, and Mitchum's taking a walk around town. The girl hasn't been downstairs, but she's all right.

I talked with the waitress who takes up her food. She keeps the door locked on Macklin, and he's been threatening to break it down. Guess he would've busted in before this if Mitchum hadn't talked him out of it. You'd better wait in the wagon a while, Sherry."

"I don't know," Sherrill said. "I can't stand much more waiting, Steve."

"It's no fun," admitted Ehlers. "But neither is getting shot in the back."

"Mitchum wouldn't take that advantage. He's too sure of himself. But Macklin, he might do anything."

"But you say Mitchum stabbed the fat man in the back?"

"Yes, but that was a little different," said Sherrill. "They couldn't risk shooting and waking up the whole camp. Mitch wouldn't take anybody from behind by choice."

"Noble character, for a renegade," Ehlers said dryly.

"I'm going in and wait at the bar," Sherrill decided. "Let 'em come to me." He pulled the brim of the borrowed campaign hat lower over his face.

"All right," agreed Ehlers. "You can watch both doors in the mirror behind the bar. I'll go in the front way and find me a table where I can observe the proceedings."

"Steve, I don't want you throwing into this," Sherrill warned.

"Don't worry, I won't," said Ehlers. "I'm a peace-loving man." He grinned, still with the cigar clamped between his teeth, and strolled off toward the front of the hotel.

CHAPTER SIXTEEN

After a few minutes Sherrill loosened the guns in their sheaths, jumped down from the wagon, and walked along the alley. The full moon was radiant as a flawless silver coin in the night-blue heavens, dimming out the near stars with its light, gliding rooftops and chimneys and cottonwood trees, whitening the gravel under Sherrill's crunching boots. A light breeze brought the smell of sage and sand, and the weird sorrowful howl of a wolf in the distance, answered by the nearby baying of village dogs. Sherrill paused for a moment to drink in the beauty of the scene, sighed and turned to the swing-doors, looking over the top into the saloon. Neither Macklin nor Mitchum was in sight, and he pushed on through.

There were ten people in the room besides the bartender. A soldier and two civilians at the bar; a man and woman at a table; a poker game in the corner was occupying the attention of four players and a spectator. As Sherrill took his stand at the bar, apart from the others, he saw in the mirror Sergeant Ehlers entering from the lobby to sit down at a central table. Sherrill ordered whiskey and left it untouched for the time being, absently tracing a diamond design on the wood with his forefinger, watching the mirror with idle interest.

The soldier at the bar kept casting drunken side-glances at Sherrill's army shirt and hat. Apparently he either wanted to talk or fight with somebody. After a while he edged closer and asked:

"You new at the post, brother?"

"No, I'm not in service any more," Sherrill said.

The private's look became instantly baleful and truculent. "Then you ain't got no right wearin' that shirt, mister!"

Sherrill, annoyed at this intrusion, managed to smile into his drink. "You want to buy me a new one? Or just take this one off me?"

The cavalryman blinked down at Sherrill's guns and gestured angrily. "You take *them* off, mister, and I'll tend to the shirt for yuh right sudden!"

Sergeant Ehlers' voice barked out behind them: "Harris! You'll shut up and tend to your own business."

Private Harris lurched about and gaped at the sergeant. "Yes, sir, Sarge. Sorry, awful sorry." He went back to his drink and grinned foolishly at Sherrill. "Didn't mean nothin' at all. No offense, mister?"

"It's all right, soldier," said Sherrill. "I'll buy another shirt when I get time."

Harris raised his glass to him, and Sherrill lifted his own and drank. The private still wanted to talk.

"'S a joker here with a whip," he confided. "Big mean-lookin' gent. Drivin' everybody crazy with that quirt. And today, you know what he done today? 'S a little old dog hangs around the hotel. Used to, I mean. Well, the pup barks at this big jasper today, and I'll be struck dead if he don't unfurl that whip. Like to cut that poor pup in half. Broke the dog's back, laid him wide open, killed him dead!" Private Harris shook his head sadly. "Terrible thing to see."

"Nice fellow," said Sherrill.

"Yeah!" growled the bartender. "That was my dog. I'm liable to load that gent's next drink with rat poison or somethin'! "

Sherrill smiled. "Maybe you won't have to do that."

Just then he saw the lank form and long, sad face of Mitchum in the mirror, moving in from the lobby. Mitchum had shaved except for the mustache drooping over his bitter mouth. Dressed in black, with that gaunt, melancholy face, he looked more than ever like a back-hills preacher. Mitchum's mournful gaze swept the saloon, dismissing the customers one by one, and returned to linger briefly on Sherrill's blue-shirted back.

Mitchum had started to retrace his steps to the lobby when all at once he wheeled about, and Sherrill saw the sudden flare and contraction of those pale, strange eyes in the glass. Swiveling smoothly from the bar, Sherrill faced him. The room went silent, and the poker game ceased as the others along the bar shifted out of the danger zone.

Mitchum's sorrowing expression never altered. "Hello, Sherry," he said. "Almost didn't recognize you in that rig. You joined the army?"

"I reckon you didn't expect to see me again, Mitch."

"That's a fact," admitted Mitchum. "Kinda thought you might've run into some Indians out there."

"I did," Sherrill said. "But my number wasn't up yet."

"Well, it sure is now." Mitchum sighed unhappily. "I reckon Cord wanted you, kid. Almost wish he'd seen you first. But long as I did, I suppose I'll have to take you."

"Don't make me cry, Preacher." Sherrill smiled, but his lips felt frozen, his cheeks starched stiff.

"Unless you wanta breeze out, Sherry?" He sounded hopeful.

Sherrill shook his head. "I've come too far for that, Mitch. And waited too long."

Mitchum sighed once more. "Too bad, kid. Always kinda liked you."

His hand flicked with the speed of light and Sherrill moved with him, moved with a fluid grace that was even faster. Mitchum's gun cleared its holster, but Sherrill's was already lined and blazing red. Mitchum fell back three uneven steps and held himself there, still trying to bring up the gun barrel, utter disbelief in his pale shocked eyes. Mitchum's gun exploded at last into the floorboards, and Sherrill blasted him again.

Mitchum doubled and bowed from the impact, stumbling back against the door jamb on jacking legs. Mitchum hung there tottering, shot to pieces but still trying to get his Colt up, still unable to believe that this could have happened to him, that he was riddled and dying on his feet. With a final convulsive jerk of his head Mitchum teetered forward and began to sag, his gun arm dropping lifeless and his knees giving slowly, until he collapsed at last with his face against the floor.

Sherrill heard Ehlers' warning cry even as he saw Cord Macklin at the bottom of the stairway just inside the lobby and switched his .44 in that direction. There came an ear-splitting crack and Sherrill's right hand went numb and useless as that whip snaked out like lightning and caught his wrist. Sherrill was reaching for his left-hand gun when a tremendous force hoisted him headlong toward Macklin, the tight-lashed quirt searing into his wrist and nearly yanking his right arm off at the shoulder. The Colt clattered to the planks from his nerveless fingers as he flew forward, his toes scarcely touching the floor.

Sherrill saw Macklin's huge fist coming as the big man hauled him in close, and ducked barely in time to take it on the skull instead of square in the face. Even there it stunned and shook him, but he felt Macklin's left-hand knuckle bones go and heard the man's gasp of pain as they collided at the foot of the stairs. The momentum carried Macklin back and down in the middle of the dimly lighted lobby, with Sherrill on top of him.

After a kicking, thrashing, heaving moment when he feared he was lost in Cord's crushing grasp, Sherrill fought his way free with fists, elbows and knees. Diving away, Sherrill scrambled to his knees, still wrist-locked by the quirt, and went again for his left-hand gun. Cord Macklin was flat on his back, holding the whip that bound them together. He pulled Sherry off balance before he could draw, lifting Sherry bodily to his feet and reeling him in like a large fish. Sherrill had never felt such terrible devastating strength and power. Macklin was sitting up now.

Recovering and rushing in to slacken the quirt that threatened to sever his right hand, Sherrill's driving knees flattened Macklin again. Cord was clawing at his legs when Sherrill stamped a boot into that broad, dark face beneath him. It would have finished an ordinary man, but Cord Macklin only brought his mighty legs around and kicked Sherrill halfway across the room.

Sherrill pitched headlong over a chair and table that crumpled under him. Bouncing off the leather couch against the wall, he sprawled back on the floor. Macklin reared to his feet, face smashed into gory ruin by Sherrill's heel but his vast strength undiminished, his broken left hand reaching for his gun as he snaked Sherrill back toward him on the hardwood.

That blasted whip, Sherrill thought fleetingly. It made a hooked fish of a man, took all the dignity and decency out of fighting. But there was too much hate between them to settle the issue in an orthodox manner in any case.

Cord Macklin was awkward with his broken hand, and Sherrill was going for his own left holster as Cord dragged him nearer. Changing tactics abruptly, Cord hurled his great bulk in to batter and wreck that lithe figure on the boards. But Sherrill swung around and got his boots up in time to catch Macklin's heavy body and propel him on overhead. Macklin tumbled with a crash that jarred the whole building and unmoored the lobby desk with a rending report.

Cord recovered with catlike quickness for such a giant, but Sherrill was up ahead of him, left hand sweeping into a draw. The Colt was half out when Cord Macklin jerked Sherry off his feet and drew him relentlessly forward, the quirt biting deep into that tortured right wrist. Sherrill's left hand flew up with the .44, but too high to shoot as Cord snagged him in savagely and clubbed him with the broken left fist.

Sherrill's head snapped, his eyes went blind from the concussion, and blood filled his mouth and streamed from his nose. Desperately he ducked and rolled under the next blow, twisting sinuously to slash his gun barrel viciously across Cord's head. It would have felled a steer, but Cord Macklin stayed upright, swaying a trifle, blood pouring from his split scalp and shattered face as they grappled and lurched back and forth in a close, furious embrace. Their blood and sweat mingled as they strained and panted for the advantage, upsetting furniture, rebounding from the walls. It required all of Sherrill's nerve, will and explosive reserve power to match the bursting boundless strength of Macklin. Then Cord suddenly lifted a cruel knee into Sherrill's groin and slugged him over the head with the loaded butt of the whip as Sherry bent over from the grinding pain.

Landing hard on his back, Sherrill slid against the base of the uprooted counter, torn in two with agony, his head reeling and expanding with vivid rocketing lights. Clinging to the .44 in his left hand, fighting to retain his senses, Sherrill writhed around onto hands and knees to face Cord. He tried to raise his left hand, but the gun was very heavy, and Macklin's bulk seemed shrouded and swimming in a fantastic stemming haze.

For the first time Cord Macklin let go of the quirt and went for his six-shooter with his good right hand. Blind and dazed as he was, Macklin got it out fast, but by that time Sherrill had made the supreme effort, and his gun was level and flaming in his left hand. Macklin rocked ponderously as the slugs struck him and drove him backward. Macklin's revolver roared in return, splintering first the desk behind Sherrill and then the ceiling.

Firing from his knees, numb right hand dangling the whip as it supported his left now, Sherrill poured lead into that vast broken, shambling hulk. The lobby was a blazing, reeking inferno as Cord Macklin floundered back in long erratic suspended staggers, snarling through his blood, trying to control his jittering gun hand. He sat down at last in the main entrance, his massive shoulders blocking the door. Macklin was still alive, but he could not get his gun up, and his final shot ripped the flooring beside his right leg.

Sherrill, teeth shining white between lacerated lips, climbed carefully upright and walked unsteadily forward, the quirt trailing unheeded from his right wrist, the Colt smoking in his left hand as he came to stand over the dying giant. Cord Macklin's black eyes, venomous to the end, glared up at Sherrill from that grotesque bloody mask of a face.

"Some of this was for Patchin, Veronica, and the rest," Sherrill told him, slowly and clearly. "But mostly, I guess, it was for me."

Cord Macklin's swollen lips snarled back from his reddened teeth and he died that way, snarling, propped awkwardly in the doorway of the Colorado Hotel in Bridger, Utah Territory.

Sherrill walked slowly back toward the desk, unwrapping the tight-wound whiplash from his wrist. Leaning on the tilted counter, he bowed his head over the blood-drenched right hand, where agony was slashing like lightning flashes. A good thing he'd worn the leather wristlet, or Cord's quirt would have cut off the hand. Well, it was over. ... It had taken an ungodly time, but it was finished. Mitchum lay dead in the saloon, Macklin in the wreckage of the lobby. Sherrill drew a long thankful breath through the weary nausea that filled him.

Then Sergeant Steve Ehlers was beside him with a bottle of whiskey and a tall glass of water. Sherrill took a deep pull from the bottle and drained the water glass. Ehlers thrust a cigarette into his mouth and applied the match. Sherrill inhaled deliberately, the smoke biting into his cut lips.

"Thanks, Steve."

"There's a doctor coming," Ehlers said. "I thought Macklin was going to take that hand right off, Sherry."

"So did I," said Sherrill. "Only the cuff saved it. That blasted whip ... I never went against anything like that."

"I never want to!" Ehlers declared with a shudder. "Gosh darndest thing I ever saw, and I've seen a lot of 'em. Well, I never want to see anything like that again. Come on over and stretch out on this couch, Sherry. You had one honey of a session."

Sherrill was lying on the couch when the doctor came to cleanse and bandage his wrist, bathe and sterilize his head and face abrasions. The leather cuff had prevented serious or permanent damage; the wrist would be all right in time.

Private Harris was among the onlookers, quite sober now. "Imagine me gettin' tough with a man like that!" marveled Harris. "Guess I better quit drinkin' as of now."

"Harris, clear these people out of here," ordered Ehlers. "Get 'em back in the barroom where they belong. The show is over."

"You betcha, Sarge," said Harris, and commenced herding the awed crowd back into the saloon.

Sherrill was dimly aware that the sheriff was there, listening to Steve Ehlers' explanation of the killings, while his deputies dragged the bodies outside and covered them with blankets on the veranda. After the sheriff left, Ehlers brought the whiskey bottle and another glass of water. Sitting up stiffly, Sherrill reached for the glass.

"Water goes better, Steve. Must've lost my taste for liquor."

Ehlers grinned and tipped the bottle to his own mouth. Wiping his lips, he glanced up the stairway. "She'll be worried, Sherry. All that shooting and racket."

"I'm going up in a minute," Sherrill said. "As soon as I feel able to make the stairs."

"Her room is down at the end of the hall on the left," Ehlers said. "Tell her the wagon train's all right, her folks are all right. A rider just came in. The Indians attacked, but they beat 'em off until the cavalry came up and routed the Cheyennes. The army's escorting the train in now."

"That's fine," Sherrill murmured. "I was worried."

Private Harris returned with Sherrill's righthand gun. "Here's the other one, Mr. Sherry. Some joker was tryin' to sneak it out for a souvenir. I'd sure be proud to shake your hand, if you don't mind."

"Glad to have you, soldier," grinned Sherrill. "Just shake it kind of easy though."

"Thanks, Mr. Sherry, thanks a lot," Harris said. "Now I'd sure like to buy you a drink."

"You can buy me one instead, Harris," said Steve Ehlers with a smile. "Sherry's got something better to do."

They saluted him and sauntered away into the saloon. After a space Sherrill rose and limped to the stairway, gripping the banister with his left hand and mounting the treads slowly. There was no elation in him. It was a good thing that Mitchum and Cord Macklin were dead, but all he felt was relief. Thank heaven it was ended at last. Sherrill never wanted to raise his guns again. All he wanted was to love and live with Molly Romney, for the rest of his days.

His boots clumped dully along the corridor, his shadow wavering under the oil lamps bracketed on the walls. His stride lengthened slightly as he neared the end of the hallway and saw the last door on the left outlined in a rectangle of light.

Sherrill rapped gently, and the door opened narrowly, then was flung wide. Molly Romney stood there with the lamplight golden behind her, gray eyes shining softly, lovely face uplifted, and her arms open to receive him.

"Sherry!" she cried with eager, happy delight. "I knew you'd come, Sherry, and I wasn't afraid. I knew the first time I ever saw you, Sherry.... I knew there wasn't anything in the world that could keep us apart."

Sherrill could not speak, but his arms closed tenderly around her, and he tasted the cool, ripe sweetness of her mouth. Then he stood holding the girl with gentle firmness and breathing in the fragrance of her lustrous dark hair.

Oddly enough, he thought of Harry Connover in that moment, and smiled over Molly's head into the soft, tremulous lamplight of her room. Harry had been right again. Harry was always right: Sherrill had found what he really wanted and needed out here on the western plains.

www.ingramcontent.com/pod-product-compliance
Lightning Source LLC
Chambersburg PA
CBHW020916180626
46816CB00007BA/2424